"Stay where you are."

Paul stopped directly in front of Allison and, for the space of a second, did nothing but look at her with burning eyes.

Allison was aware of the explosiveness of the situation. He was angry because she was wearing Oriel's dress. In his opinion, she had done the unforgivable. She knew she should try to save herself, but she couldn't make herself move.

Emotion flooded through her. She didn't know what she felt for Paul. It didn't have a name. But when he reached for her, Allison didn't hesitate.

Her body fitted perfectly against his. She could feel the strength of his muscles, the intimate warmth of his skin, the rapid rise and fall of his chest. His eyes were like black diamonds glittering in their own darkness. And when he brought his mouth close, she was ready for his kiss....

ABOUT THE AUTHOR

Ginger Chambers gets story ideas from a variety of sources. Sometimes, she starts with a specific character in mind, puts the person in a situation and watches as the action starts to evolve. Such was the case with hero Paul Sullivan in this book. Ginger was also so taken by Paul's friend Randall that she created a story just for him, #411, *Eagle on the Wind,* coming to you in October. A native Texan, Ginger lives in her California with her husband and two children.

Books by Ginger Chambers
HARLEQUIN AMERICAN ROMANCE

GINGER CHAMBERS

BIRD IN A MIRROR

Harlequin Books

TORONTO • NEW YORK • LONDON
AMSTERDAM • PARIS • SYDNEY • HAMBURG
STOCKHOLM • ATHENS • TOKYO • MILAN

Published June 1991

ISBN 0-373-16395-9

BIRD IN A MIRROR

Chapter One

Paul Sullivan sat stiffly at the table, his sculpted features rigid with pain.

"I want to see them in hell, Randall! I want to make them pay. For what they did to her. For what they did to—" He had been going to say *us* but quickly censored the word. Randall was his best friend, yet he didn't know everything.

"It's over," Randall said, trying to soothe. "Oriel can't be hurt by them any longer. She's past that now. What you have to do is try to forget."

"I *can't* forget! Not when none of them is sorry that she's dead."

Randall tried again to be the voice of reason. "You cared for her. You were practically a member of her family...I know the story! But I still say that this blind hatred is hurting you more than them. They're above feeling the same kind of pain that you do...or should I say 'below?' Whatever. It isn't doing you any good. Why don't you take a short vacation? Get away for a few weeks. You can afford it. Then, when you come back, you'll have had time to adjust. See things in perspective."

"She died in a strange place, among people who didn't know her—didn't care about her."

"She checked herself into the institute because she had a problem."

"Now she has a worse one."

"*Now* she's at rest. Let yourself rest, too!" Randall glanced restively at his watch. "I have a meeting in fifteen minutes, otherwise I'd— Possibly I can move it. Let me call Marsha and..."

"Go to your meeting. I don't need a nursemaid."

"You need something!" Randall clipped, his impatience stemming from concern. "Let's get together later this afternoon. Have a drink or something."

Paul shook his head. "I have things to do."

"Tomorrow, then," Randall urged, rising.

Paul shrugged. He didn't seem to notice when his friend walked away.

Alone with his bitter thoughts, Paul remained as oblivious to the crowded restaurant as he had been moments before upon his arrival. The difficult journey from Los Angeles to San Francisco had done nothing to ease the bleakness of his soul.

He wanted revenge. He wanted the people responsible for Oriel's death to suffer for everything they had done to her.

Slowly an awareness of the people around him worked its way into his consciousness. They were laughing and talking, getting on with their lives, untouched by the catastrophe that had just shattered his life. They had no reason to share his loss, his outrage. He had loved her! He *still* loved her! She couldn't possibly be dead!

Instinctively he reached for the drink that Randall had left untouched, downed it in a reflex action and waited for the warmth to melt some of the ice that encased his soul. But the warmth didn't come. The glass might have contained water.

The memorial service he'd attended that morning had attracted many people. Like him, some of them even mourned. But the grief shown by those closest to Oriel could easily be seen through; all they could think about was her father's will and the fact that now that it had expired, they would be free. The Bereaved Husband even intended to hold their annual house party in two weeks' time, as if nothing had happened. And they were all going to come!

Bile rose in Paul's throat at the depth of their perfidy. He hated them. Hated each and every one of them. And if, one day, he ever had the opportunity for revenge...

A vision of Oriel as he had first seen her floated into his mind. He had been at the end of a difficult journey then, too. A journey that had begun in happiness, when his parents, both musicians, had agreed to take him along on their European tour. The first month had been marvelous, his parents reserving as much time as they could to show their twelve-year-old son the wonders of London and Paris and Vienna.

Only that happiness didn't continue. Tragedy struck in the form of an air crash. Left in the care of a nurse-maid while his parents flew to the estate of a friend, Paul never saw them again. His main memory of that dark moment was of his parents' manager coming solemnly into the hotel room and the woman hired to watch over him crying unabashedly in the background.

What followed was a whirlwind of people and planes and automobiles, until at last he arrived at the huge Woodrich mansion on the outskirts of Los Angeles, which was to be his new home. A party was taking place in the great house. A birthday party. He would never forget the multitude of lights and fresh flowers and ribbons that greeted his jaded eyes. And people—mostly young people—dressed in their finest. He had felt so lost and alone, standing in the doorway in his wrinkled shorts and private school jacket with the tiny insignia embroidered on its pocket. Music played, laughter surrounded him, and all he could do was stare.

Then she appeared. To his twelve-year-old eyes, she had looked like a fairy princess with her abundance of red-gold hair, skin the color and texture of rich, smooth cream, and those long green eyes that could haunt even the most hardened man's soul. On the night of her sixteenth birthday, she had been entertaining her guests, her delicate mouth bowed into a happy smile, her beautiful face aglow. Then she looked across at him. Her smile hovered uncertainly for a moment, before breaking away from her friends, she had come to him.

"Are you Paul?" she asked curiously. Her voice was sweet and musical, like the flute his mother had played.

Unable to speak, he had merely nodded.

Her smile flashed, warming him, drawing him like a moth to the flame of her spirit.

"My name is Oriel," she said. "We're going to be great friends. Why don't you come in? My mother will be happy that you've arrived at last."

Then she extended her hand, reaching out to him.

Paul remembered staring at it and at her. He remembered hesitating. Then he placed his hand in hers, feeling the softness of her skin and the radiance of her person. And in that moment, unacknowledged but understood, he knew that he had fallen in love.

Both pleasure and pain twisted in Paul's heart as, for that moment, she was with him again—smiling at him, saying his name...

Then a voice interrupted his thoughts, dragging him back into the present, making him remember.

Resentfully Paul shot the interloper an angry look... only to have the earth suddenly lurch beneath his feet—because Oriel was standing *there*! Next to him! The same red-gold hair, the same creamy skin, the same beautiful face with those haunting green eyes. Paul stared at her in utter shock.

But instead of smiling a greeting, Oriel frowned. "Are you all right? Are you ill? Do you need help?" She spoke from what seemed a long distance away.

Paul's dark eyes continued to reflect his stupefaction while at the same time his mind whirled with the impossibility of what he saw. This couldn't be happening! Oriel was dead. She had burned in the flames of two fires—one of accident, one of cremation. She couldn't possibly be beside him now, unless...

He groped to test the reality of her being and found the substance of her arm. His hand jerked away in shocked surprise.

Oriel stepped back. "I'll—I'll get someone," she stammered.

When Paul saw that she was turning to leave, he tried to stop her. "No!" he cried, jumping up, his chair toppling over in his hurry.

Heads turned. He felt the weight of countless eyes. Yet he couldn't remove his gaze from the vision.

"Oriel?" he breathed huskily, all the love and longing he had ever felt for her wrapped into that one ragged plea.

She continued to pull away. He tried to catch up to her, but his feet seemed covered in mud—thick, cloying mud that kept him from moving properly. In his heart, panic rose. Why was she running away from him like that? Did she think he was like all the others? Uncaring? Unloving? Interested only in himself?

Strong fingers twined around his arms, checking him even as he tried to pull forward. "Hold on, friend," a deep voice cautioned.

Paul ignored the warning. "Oriel, please," he begged. He had to make her see! Had to make her understand! He *loved* her!

A man in black came up behind Oriel and moved her into such a position that Paul couldn't see her any longer. "No!" he cried, bobbing his head. "You don't understand!"

The man in black came to stand directly in front of him and was about to say something, when Paul loosened an arm and knocked him away, causing him to crash into a nearby table. Screams followed as people scrambled aside.

Soon other hands were joining the first and Paul's free arm was yanked up behind his back until tears smarted in his eyes. Muffled words were exchanged as he was bent forward and propelled along the same route that Oriel had taken.

People continued to scurry out of the way.

"Please," Paul choked. *"Please!"* he cried again, as he was whisked through the entryway and pointed toward the main exit.

"If you don't behave, I'll call the police," a voice hissed roughly in his ear.

The front doors were thrust open by the force of their bodies. Paul blinked at the brightness of the sun. Then he was unceremoniously turned, his back plastered against the restaurant's wall. He was held there for several long moments until one by one the hands let go, their owners standing away, still watchful, ready to repeat their force if need be.

The man in the dark suit glared at him. Slight of build, he barely came to the level of Paul's shoulders, but at the moment he was the one in charge.

"I'm going to explain this to you once," he said, his words grating harshly. "Leave Allison alone. She's a good girl. She doesn't cause trouble for anyone, and I'm not going to let anyone cause trouble for her. So you just be on your way and don't come back again, unless you're willing to abide by my rules. Understand?"

Paul's breaths were coming in quick inhalations as he strove to comprehend.

"Understand?" the man insisted, his anger boring into him, willing an answer.

Paul nodded jerkily, and the men relaxed their stance even more, adjusting their jackets while directing curious looks at him. All except for the man in the dark suit, who still watched him with great distrust.

As he became conscious of the crowd that had gathered on the sidewalk, a dull stain of embarrassment crept into Paul's cheeks. He hadn't been involved in a public altercation since childhood. He felt humiliated, shamed. He had made a scene in a restaurant, of all places!

But the woman had looked so much like Oriel.

It was still hard for him not to believe...

Paul escaped to the safety of his office, but no matter how hard he tried he could not escape the questions in his mind. For the remainder of the afternoon—as he endeavored to work with clients, as he attempted to concentrate on paperwork—the odd scene would not release him. Over and over it played until finally, to gain some peace, he decided to return to the restaurant. He had to know: *had* the woman looked like Oriel? Startlingly like her, from the coloring of her skin, to her hair, to the color of her eyes? Or had she merely been a figment of his imagination?

THE RESTAURANT was located only a short distance from his office. As he neared the entrance, he almost turned away. What if he was recognized? What if someone called the police? It would do his reputation no good at all to be hauled off to jail for disturbing the peace.

He continued inside, where he quickly faded behind a tall plant when he saw the man in black come hurrying by, intent on some matter of importance. The restaurant was as crowded for the evening meal as it had been at midday.

When Paul presented himself to be seated, the hostess didn't recognize him. He was shown to a section not far from the table he had occupied earlier, and as he followed the hostess's lead he glanced at the people scattered nearby. No one returned his look with undue caution.

Once he was seated he opened the menu but could not focus on it. He felt a fool, an idiot. What was he doing here?

Someone approached his table.

"Would you care for a drink before dinner, sir?"

The masculine voice was a tremendous relief. "Ah—no. No, thank you," Paul said nervously. "I'll . . . just order."

Food was the last thing he wanted. But he couldn't just sit there doing nothing.

Alone again, Paul let his gaze work casually around the room. Uneventful seconds passed and he began to relax. Tomorrow he would return for lunch, since it was possible that the woman he had seen wasn't working the evening shift. But his belief that what he had experienced had been an illusion was growing. He had desperately wanted to bring Oriel back to life. So in his mind, he had.

He settled more comfortably into his chair, actually beginning to experience a rumble of hunger, when the shock of recognition once again riveted him to his seat. *She was there . . . coming across the room! Walking straight toward him!*

A chill radiated throughout Paul's body and a light sweat broke over his skin. She was there! Oriel was there! It *hadn't* been a trick of his mind!

She stopped at a spot several tables away from him and slid a huge round serving tray onto a rack. After smiling politely at the waiting couple, she began to serve them . . . until the intensity of Paul's look was somehow transmitted and her head lifted.

It took only a second for their eyes to meet.

Paul continued to stare at her; she blinked in confusion.

Finally recognition sparked and she bobbled the steaming bowl of soup she held, splashing hot liquid onto the tablecloth and the lap of the man she was about to serve.

"Hey! Watch out!" the man yelped, jumping hastily to his feet.

The waitress didn't seem to hear him. Instead, she continued to look at Paul and breathed only a single word: *"You!"*

Chapter Two

Allison's attention jerked back to her customer.

"Clumsy idiot!" he swore as he wiped ineffectually at his slacks with his napkin. "Are you trying to maim me?"

The beautiful woman who was his companion tried to calm him, but the man would have none of it.

"Well? Aren't you going to say anything?" he demanded.

Allison apologized, her color heightened by the knowledge that the mishap had drawn so much attention. She handed the man a second napkin and quickly set about stemming the tide of drips that were falling to the floor.

Armand rushed up beside her. She felt his quick appraisal.

"I am so sorry," he apologized to the customer. "Please, I am sure it was an accident."

"When you hire incompetent help, accidents have a way of happening!" the man snapped nastily.

"Please—" Armand signaled for assistance. Another waiter hurried over. "You must let us make this up to you. Your dinner is to be at our expense. No." He held up a hand as if to ward off a protest, which was nonexistent. "I insist. In a moment everything will be as wonderful as it was before. Please resume your seat. Also send us your cleaning bill. Again, I insist."

The man slowly retook his chair. He continued to grumble, but Armand had taken the edge off his bad humor.

Allison met Armand's shiny black eyes. The wink he gave her went a long way toward relieving the knot that had developed in her stomach.

Still her hands trembled as she helped reset the table. She couldn't afford to lose this job. Not now. Not when everything was becoming so difficult.

With quick movements, matters were put right. "Is there anything more I can do?" she asked softly before departing.

"No!" came the man's terse reply.

"No, thank you," murmured his companion.

Allison hurried away, but not before looking in the direction of the man who had caused the disturbance. He was no longer seated at the nearby table. During the ensuing moments, he had disappeared.

Allison gave a small shudder. He had acted so strangely earlier, calling her by another name, that Armand had thrown him out. Why had he come back?

She hurried into the kitchen. It was time to check the progress of her other tables, but first she had to deliver coffee to the station she had promised previously.

Rebecca, a fellow waitress, was gathering desserts onto a tray. She glanced at Allison sympathetically. "That man's an ass. Don't worry about him. I've served him before—he enjoys making life difficult for the peons."

"It's not him I'm worried about," Allison replied, reaching for cups and a carafe of coffee. "Did you see that man at lunch—the one Armand threw out?"

"I couldn't help *not* seeing. Too bad he's a nutzoid. What a waste of good looks—tall and dark with great features, fabulous eyes and thick black hair!" Rebecca sighed in feigned infatuation.

"Well, he was back just now, watching me. That's why I spilled the soup."

Rebecca paused in her work, suddenly serious. "Have you told Armand? You should. He'd want to know."

"Not yet. But the man's gone now."

Rebecca lifted her tray. "You better watch out when you go home, honey. Don't walk down any dark alleys. You never can tell these days, with so many crazies on the streets. And just because he looks good doesn't mean that he is good!"

"I *never* walk down dark alleys!"

"You know what I mean." Rebecca tilted her head. "Would you like me and Ike to take you home tonight? We don't mind."

Allison hesitated for only a second. "Sure, that would be great!"

Then, with exaggerated care, she balanced her tray on her upraised hand and started for the swinging kitchen doors in Rebecca's wake. She didn't want to have another accident. Armand was supportive, but even his goodwill had a limit.

AFTER WAVING GOODBYE to the couple who had dropped her off outside the narrow doorway that led to the apartment she shared with her grandfather, Allison quickly ran up the short flight of stairs to the outside door, slipped inside, then hurried up the remaining flight of stairs to their apartment.

It was late, and from the street she could see that her grandfather's bedroom light was off, but she was still anxious to check on him. Ever since the night she had thought him sound asleep only to have the police bring him home at two in the morning, she lived in fear of it happening again. After starting off to the corner store for a carton of milk, he had wandered the streets for hours, lost and afraid, temporarily unable to remember his own name.

As quietly as she could, she opened his door. The night-light, plugged into the wall near his bed, gave a soft glow to the room. Her grandfather was lying on his side, covers up to his ear, tufts of white hair tousled on his pillow, sleeping the sleep of innocence.

Just as quietly she closed him back in. Then with a tired sigh, she hung her jacket in the hall closet and made her way into the kitchen. Nothing there beckoned her to eat, though, and she soon returned empty-handed to the small living room.

Working in a restaurant had had the opposite effect on her appetite from that which she first expected. Delivering meals to customers all day acted as a curb, not a stimulant. Not even the wonderful aromas tempted her any longer. Normally she had to force herself to eat—knowing that she must in order to keep up her strength, for herself as well as for her grandfather.

She switched on the television set and collapsed into the well-worn cushions of the overstuffed couch, only to find that the sound had been cut off. Too tired to get up, she watched as the characters on screen mouthed their way through their scenes, their lips moving, their voices unheard. One of the actresses began to silently scream and cry. Allison watched in sympathy. She knew exactly how the woman felt, because all too often recently her own muted cries for help had remained unheard. How much longer could she and her grandfather go on, with his health deteriorating and her holding down two jobs but still barely able to cover all their needs?

Faced with the monumental task of it all, her eyes flickered shut on a buildup of tears. But a moment later, forcibly dry-eyed, they reopened with fresh determination. When she had needed loving care most, her grandfather had provided it. Now it was her turn to pay him back, and she wasn't going to shirk her responsibility.

When the time came, she would ask for steady overtime work at the restaurant, not just the sporadic extra hours she managed now. The restaurant always needed experienced staff; she knew she would be able to talk Armand around. The problem was that if they were to the point of needing more money, it meant that her grandfather would require that much more care. More than Mrs. Beaumont, their next-door neighbor, looking in on him frequently during the day. He would need constant monitoring, for his own protection.

Allison winced at the memory of the kitchen fire Mrs. Beaumont had miraculously walked in on just the previous week. Her grandfather had been cowering near the refrigerator, afraid and whimpering, not knowing how to extinguish the blaze in the skillet.

They had removed the knobs from the stove after that and Mrs. Beaumont started having her grandfather over to her apartment for his meals. But Mrs. Beaumont was not in the best of health herself. How much longer could they impose?

Allison jerked to her feet, rejecting an unwelcome thought. She would *not* put her grandfather in a nursing home. She would not! Something would work out. It *had* to!

No longer able to be willed away, tears of exhaustion and worry rolled down over her cheeks. Today had not been easy. So many people had been so demanding. It had even been difficult in the bookshop where she worked mornings. When she hadn't instantly known the title of a certain book after a vague, rambling description, the customer blamed her. As if she should know everything! As if she had the luxury of time to read! And Dexter Wheeler wasn't as understanding as Armand. He became irritated if she made even the smallest mistake.

Surely tomorrow would be a better day. She at least had to tell herself that, didn't she?

PAUL KICKED THE COVERS from his legs and swung his feet to the floor. Sleep was impossible. All he could think about was the woman from the restaurant. Repeatedly his mind replayed the picture he held of her, which continued to blend with his image of Oriel. Oriel before life had turned against her. Oriel as a young woman—sweet and innocent and giving.

It had taken hours for his emotions to settle after their second encounter. Hours in which instinct had grappled with intellect and he could clearly tell himself that she wasn't Oriel come mysteriously back to life. That she was an individual in her own right—living and breathing—with her own cares and concerns, her own life.

If he didn't know better, he might suspect that she was a plant. There was no love lost between him and the others who made up Oriel's closest circle of friends. They knew exactly what he thought of them; he had made his feelings abundantly clear. He wouldn't put it past any one of them to have hired the woman to act the part so that—

Paul became very still, his last thought echoing in his mind. At first the idea was like a curling wisp of smoke, hard to capture, harder even to see. Then slowly it began to take shape: *No one was playing a trick on him ... but it was possible that he could play a trick on someone else. On a* number *of someone elses!*

"YOU'RE MAD!" Randall Peters decreed, his clean-cut features plainly appalled as he looked at the man sitting so calmly across from his desk. "You've flipped your lid! Popped your cork! Snagged your rip cord! *It won't work.* You can't possibly expect it to. They won't believe you!"

"I'll make them believe me," Paul said unequivocally.

"They'll check! They're not stupid."

"Let them."

"What will happen when they discover the truth? Have you thought about that? How long do you think this can last? One day? Two?"

"I'll fix things so it will last longer," Paul assured. Then hardening his jaw, he continued, "I want to make them suffer, Randall. I want to make them wonder if the nightmare is ever going to end. Each one thinks that they're going to get what they want out of this—won't they be surprised to find that they're not?"

Randall raked a hand through his light brown hair. "You could get into a lot of trouble for this, Paul. Think about it!"

Paul's dark eyes didn't waver. "I've thought of little else. I'm not out to cheat them, Randall, just delay them."

"What about the girl? Do you think she's just going to meekly agree? How do you plan to get her to do it? You don't even know her."

"I was going to let you worry about that."

"What?"

"You're going to talk to her. Not me."

Randall started shaking his head before Paul had finished speaking. "Oh, no. No, I'm not. I'm not going to get involved in this."

"You already are."

Randall continued to shake his head.

Paul said, "She won't talk to me. She probably thinks I'm crazy."

"Which you are!"

"It's simple." Paul leaned forward. "You put it to her as a job. A job that's a little unusual, but a job all the same. Which, in reality, it is."

"I won't do it," Randall said.

Paul's conscience stirred at what he was about to do, but not enough to silence him. A perfect opportunity had been presented and he was not about to waste it. "You owe me, Randall," he reminded quietly.

An electrified tension vibrated in the air between the two men.

"You're holding me to that? Now?" Randall challenged. "A short time ago I remember you telling me to forget about it."

Paul made no reply, he merely waited.

Finally Randall leaned back in his chair, his features stiff, the expression in his light eyes flat. "All right," he agreed. "I'll get her here. I'll even tell her you want to offer her a job. But that's as far as I go. You have to do the rest of your dirty work yourself. I won't be a part of it."

"I'll testify on your behalf."

Randall ignored his friend's derisive answer. "I've been your friend for a long time, Paul. I'll always be your friend. But there's a line that I won't cross, not even for you. You're not yourself right now. Your judgment is skewed all to hell and you don't care who you hurt. But one day you will care. And when that time comes, I hope you won't have to face too many regrets."

Paul continued to sit calmly. Nothing could make him change his mind. Revenge was sweet, or so the saying promised. He intended to find out.

THAT EVENING AS ALLISON loaded yet another tray in the restaurant's kitchen, she listened to Rebecca's dream of how she would like to spend her free Saturday.

"I'd go to one of those spas," she said. "You know, get my hair done, have one of those facial packs applied, then lie down and let someone with magic fingers give me a full-body massage . . . from my neck all

the way down to my toes. Especially my toes! After
today, I think my feet are going to fall off! I wonder
what it costs to go to one of those places, one of those
health farms?'' Then she laughed at the picture her
words called forth. ''That sounds like everyone should
come away with a carton of eggs and a crock of but-
ter, doesn't it? Instead of a beautiful face and a fabulous figure.''

Allison chuckled at her friend's quip, and she was
still smiling as she moved through the swinging kitchen
doors on her way to one of her tables. She wished she
could experience something as relaxing as a massage
on Saturday, but in all likelihood she would be working. Armand had asked her to take the evening shift
again tonight and had mentioned the possibility of her
coming in on Saturday, as well. And considering how
badly they needed the money, she would do it. Any
extra amount would be welcome. Her only difficulty
was in finding time to talk to Mrs. Beaumont to be
sure that she would be available to check on her
grandfather that day.

She serviced the table at the far end of her station,
then noticed that a new customer had been added to
one not far away, causing her to divert from her intended path.

''Would you care for something to drink before you
order?'' she asked, repeating her usual question.

The man lowered his menu and gave her the oddest
look. He seemed more than a little ill at ease. ''I hope
you don't think I'm being too presumptuous—'' he
began.

Allison's internal warning system activated.

"—but I have a friend," he continued, "who was wondering if you'd be interested in a position he has to offer."

"I already have a position," Allison said.

"It's a very special job," the man explained.

"Would you like a drink, sir?" she tried again. She didn't want to create another scene or spark another complaint.

"He's willing to pay a lot of money," the man went on.

Allison turned away.

"No, wait!" the man cried, drawing the attention of diners at a nearby table. His voice immediately softened. "Look . . . I'm a lawyer." He reached inside his pocket for his card. Allison glanced at it suspiciously. She read his name and the address of his office which was located in a building known for its elite tenants. "What kind of job?" she asked, frowning. "Why doesn't he ask me himself?"

The man smiled, a quick pull of his lips. "I'm acting as his intermediary, to set up the appointment."

"You didn't say what kind of job it is."

"I'd rather that he explain."

"Tell him to keep it," she dismissed.

"It truly does involve a lot of money." He then named a sum for a short period of time that caused Allison's eyes to widen.

He gauged her reaction and pressed his advantage. "You're free to accept or reject the offer. The decision will be yours. All my friend asks is that you meet with him to discuss it.''

Allison didn't know what to say. Under ordinary circumstances she wouldn't even consider the idea. Not for any amount of money. But these were not ordinary times. ''Where would we meet?'' she asked, telling herself that she was foolish, but also telling herself that it wouldn't hurt to listen.

''In my office.''

''Will you be there?''

''If you like.''

Allison hesitated. She was afraid that no good would come of such a meeting. But in the end she said, ''All right.''

Once again the man smiled tightly. ''What time tomorrow afternoon is good for you?''

''I break at three. I usually—'' She stopped. She didn't need to tell him that she usually went home to check on her grandfather.

''Then three o'clock it is.'' He extended the card. ''You probably should have this.''

Allison slipped the card into her uniform pocket and after an awkward moment took his order for a drink. She then returned to the kitchen in something of a daze.

Chapter Three

"I want your word, Paul. She gets a choice. I told her she would, and I meant it. If she turns you down, you're not going to press her. Correct?"

"Of course not."

"I mean it. I promised."

Paul sat back in the chair. He wanted very much to give the outward impression of complete control. Inside, though, his nerves were jumping with tension. He was like a stallion at the gate, quivering to be away. He didn't want to wait. He didn't want to have to go through any more preparation. The woman would do it. She had to!

He gave a terse nod.

Randall had to be satisfied with that. He looked at his watch and paced back to his desk. It was a little after three.

A moment later a light tap sounded on the door and both men's heads snapped around.

"Your three o'clock appointment, Mr. Peters," Randall's secretary announced as she stepped back out of the way to allow the visitor to pass.

As the woman from the restaurant entered the room, Paul was again struck by her uncanny resemblance to Oriel. Except now, more prepared, he could see that she was thinner than Oriel and that she also lacked the spark that had been so much a part of Oriel's personality. Still, that was all right. He wanted her to pretend to be Oriel's sister, not Oriel herself. If there were differences, it was all to the good, especially considering the plan he had come up with to explain Magda's whereabouts for the past eight years.

As soon as she saw him the woman stopped. "What is this?" she demanded before quickly turning on her heel. When Paul lunged after her, barring her exit, she froze.

For a moment, being so close to her and looking into those familiar green eyes, Paul was mesmerized. Against his will he was transported to other times, other places. He could see Oriel moving, hear her talking. Then mentally he shook himself and hurried into speech.

"I asked Randall to arrange this meeting because I didn't want to frighten you. I have a job to offer. One I'm prepared to pay quite nicely for. I believe Randall quoted a figure?"

Paul purposefully kept his expression nonthreatening as he motioned to the partially open door. "This is private. May I?"

Her body remained tensed, poised for flight. But after a moment she gave a jerky nod.

Paul saw her to a chair.

"I also believe you've been told that you're free to refuse my offer? Well, that's true, you are. But I doubt you'll want to after you hear how easy the work will be, Miss—ah . . ."

"Williams. Allison Williams," she supplied.

"Easy work," he repeated. "What I want is for you to attend a house party where you'll be wearing pretty clothes and mixing with interesting people. That doesn't sound too difficult, does it?" He attempted a smile he didn't feel. She didn't respond. "There are just three requirements," he continued. "You have to say what I tell you, act the way I tell you and learn a history you can't be shaken from."

"Who am I pretending to be?" she asked, catching on quickly.

Paul approved. Her quickness meant that she would be a fast learner.

"A woman by the name of Magda Richards." He watched to see if the name was familiar to her. While waiting for time to pass until this meeting, an unwelcome thought had occurred to him: was it possible that somehow she actually was related to Oriel? Another bastard child of Damien Woodrich? Or the real Magda Richards, come to this city without anyone's knowledge? He was relieved when she paid the name no particular notice.

"Why me?" she asked, frowning.

"Because of the way you look."

The woman tilted her chin slightly. "Where is she, then—the real Magda Richards?"

"No one knows. Speculation is that she's dead."

"Then—"

Paul held up an arresting hand. "You'll learn more only if you agree. Will you do it? I assure you, I plan nothing illegal."

The woman was wearing her waitress uniform: a neat navy blue dress with white collar and cuffs and a little gold pin engraved with her name, perched above the small pocket on the bodice.

"You'd want me to do this for a month?" she asked.

"There's always that possibility, but more than likely it will be only a few weeks. If it's less time, though, you'll still get paid the full amount."

"Here in the city?"

"No. You'll have to be prepared to travel. Not far— but definitely not in the city."

She was already shaking her head. "No. No, I can't. I'm sorry, but I can't leave San Francisco."

Paul leaned forward, placing his hands on either arm of her chair. "I'll double the price," he said softly.

Randall stirred. Paul saw him from the corner of his eye, but he didn't withdraw his gaze from the woman.

She continued to shake her head.

"I'll triple it," he said even softer. He would *make* her agree, no matter what it took!

Randall strode away from his desk. "Paul!" he cautioned shortly.

Paul ignored him. "Triple," he repeated, this time naming the sum. "Think about it. That's a lot of money for just standing around and having a good time. Think what you can do with it—buy a new wardrobe, take a holiday—a long holiday—to anywhere you want."

Randall grabbed hold of his arm. "You're bullying her, Paul!"

Paul rounded angrily on his friend, his hands automatically closing into fists, his eyes flashing a reckless challenge. Then slowly he forced himself to ease up. He couldn't believe how close he had come to striking out! The thought shamed him, but he couldn't back away from what he had to do. Not for Randall. Not for anyone.

The woman drew shakily to her feet, unavoidably aware of the volatility of the situation. "I—I have to think about it," she murmured.

"Yes, do that!" Randall urged.

Paul said coldly, "You have until five o'clock tomorrow evening. Call me at this number." He handed her a card.

The woman nodded.

Once they were alone, the two men again faced each other.

"You're making a terrible mistake," Randall warned.

"And you're butting in where you don't belong! You *want* her to turn me down, don't you?"

"I do."

"Some friend you are!"

"Yes . . . yes, I am! Or at least I'm trying to be! If you were standing in front of a runaway train, you'd want me to pull you out of the way, wouldn't you?"

"I'm not standing in front of a train!"

"Maybe it's invisible!"

"Now you're the one who's crazy!"

"You can tell yourself that all you want, Paul, but you know it's not the truth!"

Paul stared at his friend for a long moment before silently turning to leave.

ALLISON WORKED BOTH the remainder of the afternoon and the previously arranged night shift in a state of distraction. Somehow she got everyone's order right and had no accidents, but that was only because she had shifted into automatic. Her conscious mind was definitely not on her job.

Whenever she thought of the amount of money the man had offered, her stomach lurched. What she could do with that money! He had said something about a vacation—that was a joke. Instead, if she was careful, it would insure that she and her grandfather would have a financial cushion for at least six months. Six months! Days and days free of money worries. She could afford to take some time off to bring her grandfather to the beach, to take him to the zoo. Even in his uncertain state, he would enjoy a treat.

But to impersonate someone. No matter what the man claimed, wasn't that against the law? Even if it was legal, was it ethical? Why did he want her to do it? What was his motive? Not to mention the fact that she might have to be away for a full month.

Allison stuffed her hands into the pockets of her lightweight coat as she hurried down the street. Even after midnight a number of people were on the sidewalk, still moving from entertainment to entertainment. Keeping well into the light, away from walls and alleyways, she blended in as best she could with the revelers. It was not the most comfortable thing in the world to be out on her own this late at night, but if she were to work the evening shift regularly, she would have to get used to it. The idea didn't appeal.

With a silent breath of relief she let herself into the communal doorway of her tiny apartment building, then hurried up the steps. But before she could turn her key in the lock, Mrs. Beaumont rushed out of the apartment opposite. She must have been listening for her arrival.

"Oh, my dear. I'm so glad you're here!" the older woman cried.

Agitation showed on her lined face, causing fear to shoot through Allison's soul.

"Is it Grandfather?" she asked quickly. "Has something happened to him?"

The woman instantly shook her white head. "Oh, no. No. I didn't mean to make you think—" She started again. "No, it's my nephew. He's been hurt in an accident at work and I have to go stay with his little boy. Both of Bobby's legs are broken, and possibly his back. Something fell on him. Madeline is almost beside herself with worry. I was afraid I was going to have to leave before you got home, and I didn't want to do that." She paused. "My dear, I'm not sure how long this is going to take. It could be *weeks* before I get back. I'm so sorry."

Allison's compassion for her neighbor was tempered by her realization of how this was going to affect her grandfather...and herself. Still she patted the older woman's arm and tried to give comfort. "It's all right, Mrs. Beaumont. You can't help it. When your family needs you, you have to go."

"But I feel so terrible deserting you!"

"Well, don't. Everything will be just fine. I'm—I'm going to start a new job soon. One that will bring in a lot more money, so I'll be able to hire someone to take care of grandfather full-time."

"But that will be so expensive!"

Allison smiled bravely. Her six months' grace was rapidly deteriorating, but if it had to be, it had to be. During the past several years she had learned that there were times when you just had to stop fighting the inevitable and work with it. "Don't worry," she assured. "Everything will be fine."

Mrs. Beaumont was greatly relieved.

After wishing the nephew a speedy recovery, Allison let herself into her apartment then leaned back against the closed door. She had no choice now. Circumstance had taken the matter out of her hands. She would have to accept the man's proposition.

"HOW'RE YOU DOIN', girlie?" her grandfather greeted the next morning. Allison had already called the bookstore and told Dexter that she wouldn't be in that day. He didn't like it, but he agreed when she told him that she had no one to stay with her grandfather. She had yet to call Armand.

Her smile was tender as she met her grandfather's gaze. "I'm fine. How about you?"

Her grandfather had neglected to take his pajama top off before slipping into his best suit jacket. The matching slacks were belted but unzipped. The tail of his pajama top stuck out the fly. His hair was a nimbus of thinning white tufts sticking out around his head in disarray.

"I'm fine...fine," the old man claimed.

"You planning on going somewhere?" Allison asked.

"Got to get to work. I'm late. I overslept."

"You have the day off, Granddad," she reminded. "Don't you remember? Mr. Hopkins gave you the day off today." Each morning her grandfather "dressed" for work and each morning she gave him the same excuse, which he accepted happily.

"Oh, yes. That's right. That's right." As usual he shed his jacket, arranging it carefully on the back of his favorite chair before he sat down and waited. For what, Allison never knew. He didn't look at anything, he didn't expect anything or particularly want conversation. He was very much a participant in his own internal world.

To see him in so sad a state nearly broke Allison's heart. He had deteriorated so rapidly since his first series of small strokes a couple of years before. Prior to that he had been so strong. Strong of spirit, strong of body, strong of mind. When his only son had appeared one night to say that he could no longer care for her nine-year-old self, her grandfather had taken her in. The visit was supposed to be for a few weeks, but months had lapsed into years, and after a time neither spoke of a day of parting.

Her grandfather had been a crusty old baggage, then—set in his ways, unused to having children around. He had demanded that Allison conform to his methods. For a time there had been trouble. She had rebelled, hurt deeply by her father's abandonment. But her grandfather had eventually gotten around her. She didn't remember the exact moment when love had blossomed between them, but when it did it was so strong that it could never be broken. Which it still was, even if she was the one doing most of the active loving now.

Her grandfather didn't notice that she remained home from work. The occurrence was just accepted. And when she prepared his lunch instead of Mrs. Beaumont, he didn't question that fact either. In some ways he was like a child again, innocently accepting of the world and the people who inhabited it.

After lunch, when he lay down for a nap, Allison made a series of calls. Then finally she dialed the number on the man's business card.

"Yes?" he clipped when she was put through. Short and to the point.

She steadied the phone against her ear. "Mr. Sullivan? This is Allison Williams. I've—I've decided to accept your offer. On one condition."

Silence greeted her announcement. She knew that she might be playing a fool's game. He could tell her to go to hell, and that would be that. But after making calls to a number of nursing agencies in the city, she had discovered just how expensive they were. It was imperative that she at least make an effort to preserve as much as she could of her six months' grace.

"And what might that be?" he asked. His voice was smooth, ironic, as if he already knew what she was going to say.

"I—I have to have more money. I'm sorry, but I need it for my grandfather. He's ill and . . ."

"How much?" he cut in.

"Another thousand?"

"Would two be better?"

Allison's palms began to sweat. "Yes, but . . ."

"Consider it done."

Her heart jumped with joy. Then reality set in. Exactly what was she committing herself to? He had given her so little information. Could she get into any kind of trouble by helping him? Would she be safe?

"You're still hesitating?" he probed.

Allison swallowed. "I need to know more about the job. What I'm to do. I can't just . . ."

"Come to my office at five-thirty. We might as well get started."

"I can't. Not today. I need this weekend to . . . to settle some things." She would spend the time interviewing nurses and setting up a schedule for her grandfather's care. "And— And I want half of the money up front," she added.

Her demand was met with stony silence. Finally he asked, "Have you been talking with Mr. Peters?"

Allison frowned. She couldn't place who he was talking about. Then she remembered that Peters was his friend's last name. "No," she replied.

"I just wondered. All right, I'll have half the money waiting for you on Monday morning. At nine?"

"Yes."

"I suppose you want cash?"

"Yes."

"Somehow I suspected that."

He hung up, leaving Allison clinging to a lifeless line.

PAUL SAT BACK IN HIS CHAIR and smiled with cold satisfaction. He shouldn't have worried. All too many people in today's world were swayed by greed. Pile it up high enough and anything could be made to happen.

He laughed when he thought of the way she had demanded more money—her excuse. Triple the original offer wasn't good enough for her. She wanted more. What she didn't realize was that he would have been willing to go even higher. As it was, the amount would put a healthy dent in his savings, but what was money when it was going to such a worthy cause? The best of worthy causes: revenge.

He couldn't wait to see all their faces when he introduced Allison Williams as Magda Richards, Oriel's long-lost half sister. Even Oriel had given up finding her. A few sporadic letters postmarked from an island in the Caribbean where she lived with her mother were little enough to go on. Oriel had commissioned a search after their father's death, but all it yielded were rumors of Magda's death until Oriel lost interest in the search. If Magda turned up alive now, the happy plans that everyone was making would be crushed. The way Damien Woodrich's will was crafted, Magda would be next in line to inherit after Oriel. *Magda*, not them!

Still smiling coldly, Paul retrieved the sheaf of papers he had been reading before the telephone interrupted him. But his thoughts soon returned to Allison Williams.

She had nerve, he had to give her that. But an ailing grandfather? Couldn't she have come up with something a little more original than that!

Chapter Four

Magda Richards . . . Magda Richards . . .

That was who she was now. She had to keep saying the name over and over until it became second nature. And she had to remember a rather complicated history. She had to claim a knowledge that even the woman she was pretending to be had never had.

Allison gazed at herself in the mirror. Paul Sullivan had shown her a photograph of the woman he had mistaken her for at the restaurant. Her name was Oriel, the name she remembered him murmuring so brokenly the first time she had seen him. And she had been amazed at the resemblance. She could quite easily be the woman's younger sister.

With a sense of awe, Allison ran a finger over her features. As a child she had heard speculation that everyone in the world had a double, but she had never believed it. Until now.

Did the woman's real younger sister look as much like Oriel as she did herself? She had asked, but Paul Sullivan claimed not to know. He had never met her.

Allison stood away from the mirror and walked to the window that overlooked a classically beautiful street in San Francisco's Marina District. From this position she could see a wide expanse of San Francisco Bay. At the moment a giant cruise ship was churning its way toward the Golden Gate, then on to the free expanse of the sea. As she watched, it proceeded with the surety of many passages...a surety that she wished she could share.

A light tap sounded on her door causing her to spin around guiltily. Her caller could be only one person: the man in whose apartment she was now staying, the man who was paying such an exorbitant fee to have her spend every waking moment concentrating on only one thing, her new personality as Magda Richards—all done in the name of revenge.

Allison called for him to enter.

An entire week had passed since she had come to study her part—to *become* Magda—and through a great deal of hard work she was very close to mastering that goal. But in that same week she had gathered very little information about Paul Sullivan himself. He remained an enigma. From the moment they first entered the apartment he had held himself aloof, talking to her only when instructing her and absenting himself from her presence at all other times.

He eyed her critically as he came into the room. Allison shifted uneasily under his gaze.

"How old are you?" he demanded, placing her immediately into the role of student.

"Twenty-two," she lied.

"And where have you been for the past eight years? Why has no one heard from you?"

"In the convent of Our Lady of Mercy on the island of Marabu in the Caribbean. My mother sent me there the week before she died. No one's heard from me since because that was the way my mother wanted it. She was afraid of my father . . . she didn't want him to know where I was. The sisters were sworn to secrecy."

"What was your mother's name?"

"Amelia Richards."

"And your father?"

"My father was Damien Woodrich. I was the result of an illicit affair between him and my mother when she was barely nineteen. She worked in his office and he took advantage of her. When he discovered that she was pregnant, he wanted her to have an abortion, but she wouldn't do it. After I was born, he decided that he wanted to bring me up as his child along with his other daughter. But my mother wouldn't let him have me, and that made him angry. She was frightened of the power that he had over people—afraid that he might be able to gain his way. Her parents lived on a tiny island in the Caribbean and that's where we fled. My grandparents died a few years later, which left me and my mother alone."

"Oriel?" he prompted.

"Oriel," she parroted, "is—was—my sister. We exchanged letters several times when I was young. Then we lost contact . . . until a few months ago when a letter was smuggled in to me at the convent. I don't know how she learned where I was, but she did. She told me that our father was dead and I didn't have anything to fear, but by that time I was happy in the convent. I liked the quiet life—the sisters were like mothers to me. It was all I had known for so long that I didn't want to give it up. Oriel and I started to correspond. She promised to respect my desire to keep my whereabouts a secret. Since our father had lived a rather notorious life, she didn't want reporters bothering me. I wrote to a special post-office box that she rented—and she, in turn, burned each letter she received from me immediately after she read it.''

He nodded as he sat in a damask-covered chair. "How did you learn of her death?" he quizzed.

"I read about it in a newspaper. Marabu is isolated, but it's not totally off the map."

He smiled slightly. "Good. I like that."

Allison was proud of her extrapolation. After a week, she was beginning to gain an insight into the woman she was to play. It was like being an actress: she had a character, she had certain lines to speak, but turning Magda into flesh and blood was her responsibility. Sometimes, as now, when she had gained Paul Sullivan's approval, she felt sure of her ability to carry off the act. At other times, though, doubts would surface. It was one thing to repeat lines when there was relatively little pressure, but to actually be among the people she was supposed to fool... It would be so easy to get mixed up. To make mistakes.

"What do you want now? Why are you here?" His dark eyes showed no emotion beyond his questioning.

"To decide what to do with my inheritance. I'm not sure if I want it."

"But that would take the instincts of a saint!" he exclaimed, pretending to the shock the others would experience.

"The sisters taught me that money isn't everything," she answered primly. "So did my mother. And I'm thinking of becoming a sister myself."

"But you're not sure?" he pressed.

"No." Then she smiled as he had instructed her to do when challenged in this way. A small butterwouldn't-melt-in-her-mouth kind of smile that would keep them guessing. "I want to think about it for a while."

"Perfect," he approved, flashing a smile. "You're a quick study. We shouldn't have any problem being ready for the twentieth."

"Is that when the house party begins?"

He gave a short nod. Then without another word, he got up to leave.

From past experience, Allison knew that in all likelihood this would be the last time she would see him that day. She called quickly, "Mr. Sullivan!"

He turned, frowning.

"I'd like to leave the apartment for a little while this afternoon. Since we're through early I thought . . ."

"What for?" he clipped.

"To see someone. I've been here for an entire week and I've not had even a few minutes off."

No vestige of approval remained in the dark glitter of his eyes. "I'm paying for all your time this month. I want you to be immersed in this part. If you meet people you know you'll revert to the person you once were, not the person I want you to become. So the answer is no—I don't want you to leave here, not for any reason."

As Rebecca had said what seemed ages ago, he was a handsome man. Extremely handsome. Besides being physically attractive with his dark hair and dark eyes and his finely crafted features, his grooming was keyed to perfection. Never a hair was out of place, never a speck of dirt showed on his shirt or jacket, never a slip of his tongue. He was sure in what he wanted, especially in what he wanted from her. If only he were a little easier to deal with!

"A person is due some time off," she persisted. "It's my right." She very badly wanted to see her grandfather, to talk to him, to let him know that she still loved him. A hurried telephone call to the nurse on duty just wasn't enough.

"I don't work you constantly," Paul Sullivan denied. "You have free time."

"To do what? To stare at these four walls?"

A shadow of a smile passed over his features. "Think of it as coins, clicking in a meter. Then it won't seem so bad."

Allison's frustration grew. "I'm not some kind of machine!" she cried. "I have a life! Someone I love!"

He didn't budge. "Take him to Marabu with you when you're done with this. Have a romantic holiday. But that's then . . . not now!"

"Why do you hate them all so much?" she suddenly demanded, propelled into rashness by his obstinate behavior. "Why are you so determined to hurt them? If you're going to use me, I have the right to know."

"My reasons are my own," he said coldly. "You're here to do a job. Nothing more."

"I still insist on some time out—a half hour, even! I won't forget the person I'm supposed to be. I'll step back into character the second I return."

"No!" he returned shortly.

The doorbell broke into their disagreement. It rang a second time before Paul Sullivan swung angrily away from her to answer it.

"THINGS NOT GOING so well?" Randall asked after taking one look at Paul's stiff back and tightly held lips.

Paul growled a short greeting and motioned his friend into the living room. "Everything's fine. Perfectly fine. She absorbs information like a sponge."

"Then what's the matter? You look like you've just been in a fight."

"She wants some time off."

"Let her have it."

Paul's frown deepened. "No."

"Why not?" Randall asked.

Paul threw him an exasperated look. "I don't need you to start questioning my reasoning as well!"

"If you remember, I've questioned your reasoning from the beginning. And I'll continue to question it all the while you're doing this. Your hatred is consuming you, Paul. Turning you into someone I hardly know anymore. Let go of it. Let go of this idea. Pay the woman and tell her to leave. You'll be out some money, but you'll be a lot better off in the end."

Paul glared at him. "Did you come here to deliver a lecture? Because if you did, you can leave now."

"I didn't come here to deliv—"

"Just to feel superior, then," Paul interrupted. "Is that it? You have a bad habit, Randall. You think you're always right."

By now Randall's back was as stiff as Paul's. "Obviously I came at the wrong time. Call me when this is over, okay? Until then—"

"Until then, what?"

"Until then, you can—" Randall cut off the words, took a deep breath, then turned away, shaking his head.

He was at the door when Paul stopped him. "Randall?"

Randall turned.

Paul ran a hand through his dark hair; his expression was regretful, disturbed. "I didn't mean— Things are just— I'm sorry. I think what I need is a break. But

I don't trust her not to leave. Do me a favor, will you, and stay with her? I won't be gone long, no more than an hour.''

Randall looked at him curiously. ''You want me to baby-sit?''

''She's not a baby.''

''*I* know that. But I'm not so sure about you.''

Paul's testiness returned. ''I have to keep her isolated! It's important. Trust me!''

''I don't trust you at all right now,'' Randall said with brutal honesty but softened the sting with a smile. ''But I'll stay with her if you want. If you've been as friendly to her as you've been to me, the poor thing's in desperate need of a change of company. No wonder she wants to escape.''

''You're a real buddy, Randall. I won't forget this.''

''You've told me that before. I didn't like the way you said it then, and I'm not sure if I like the way you're saying it now.''

''She's in the guest room,'' Paul said, stepping quickly to the door. He then closed himself outside, with what looked like more than a little relief.

ALLISON HURRIED TO FIND her purse. She had heard voices, then the front door closed, then nothing followed except quiet. Someone must have persuaded him to go out...which was exactly what she was going to do! She didn't care if he got angry. She didn't care if he threatened to fire her. With one week left until his plan went into effect, she was on fairly safe ground.

He needed her as badly as she needed the job. Anyway, a quick visit to her grandfather was worth the risk.

She was at the base of the stairs, just off the entryway passage, when a voice seemed to come from out of nowhere. "Going somewhere, sweetheart?" it asked with droll amusement.

Allison almost jumped out of her skin. She turned to see a man standing in the archway to the living room, his pleasant features creased into a smile.

"I've always wanted to say that," he said. *"Going somewhere, sweetheart?"* It was a more than credible imitation of Humphrey Bogart.

Allison smiled uncertainly at Randall Peters. She hadn't expected to see him again. She glanced into the room behind him.

"Paul's stepped out," he explained. "He asked me to, ah—well—"

"Keep me here?" she supplied.

The man grinned unevenly. "Well...yes."

Allison closed her eyes. She felt equal portions of disappointment and rage.

Randall's smile broadened. "I'm not as much of an ogre as he is, though. Would you like to go for a walk?"

Allison hesitated only a second before nodding. She wanted to see her grandfather, but if that wasn't possible she would take the next best thing. She had worked extremely hard over the past week; she badly needed a change of scene.

Randall stepped back into the living room to leave Paul a note. "We don't want him freaking out," he murmured as he rummaged in the top drawer of a stately rolltop desk for both pen and paper.

When the front door opened and the breath of freedom washed over her, Allison realized how trapped she had felt.

By mutual consent they turned to walk the few short blocks to the bay.

Allison glanced surreptitiously at the man by her side. In comparison to Paul Sullivan's austere countenance, he too was a breath of freedom. Good humor marked his comfortable features and his gray eyes held a confident outlook on the world. He seemed the exact opposite of his friend. Yet they remained close.

"You don't approve of what he's doing, do you?" she asked as they waited at a traffic light.

Randall watched cars whiz by on the street. "Paul's a very determined person at the moment," he murmured judiciously.

"And you don't approve of determination?"

"Not when it springs from twisted reasoning."

When the way was clear they stepped away from the curb. "What was Oriel to him?" Allison asked, surprising herself. She had wanted to get away from Paul Sullivan's obsession, and here she was delving into it again. "Was she his wife? His girlfriend?"

"What has he told you about her?" Randall spared her a quick glance before returning his gaze to the panorama that was unfolding before them as they drew closer to their destination. On the left was the Golden Gate Bridge, looking close enough to touch. Before them the glorious bay. Across the water was Sausalito, nestled in the golden hills. And all the while clear, pale sunlight played on the sailboats bobbing in the distance.

"He showed me a picture of her. I do look like her. I couldn't believe it at first! It was almost like seeing myself, only—"

"Only what?"

"Well, she was older. And there was something in her face, in her eyes, an expression." She shrugged. "Something . . . unsettling."

Randall took her arm as a group of tourists, trying to take a picture of several of their members with the Golden Gate Bridge in the background, spread out over the entire sidewalk.

"Paul's parents were musicians," he explained. "From the time he was born he traveled with them. When he was twelve, they were killed. His mother and Oriel's mother were best friends, almost like sisters though they rarely saw each other after they married. They lived on different coasts. Paul went to live with Oriel's family because he had no one else. That's how it all began."

Allison was reminded of her own loss. She didn't know which was worse: losing a parent through death or through abandonment. She'd experienced both. But at least she'd had some hope of seeing her father again. For the first year or two. After that—

Randall continued, "Oriel was an interesting person. I never met her, but I've seen pictures of her. She spent most of her life in southern California. Her father had numerous business interests there and a couple of homes. When her father died, she became his legal heir." He glanced at her. "You know that Magda was illegitimate."

Allison nodded.

He went on: "Oriel was surrounded by a close circle of her father's friends. Damien Woodrich was a powerful man . . . rather Machiavellian in the classical sense of the word. He liked to use his wealth and power to make people do as he said. He enjoyed gaining a hold and not letting go. He wasn't very nice."

"I'd already decided that for myself," Allison said. "My mother—Magda's mother—had to go into hiding in order to keep her child away from him. She was afraid of him."

"That's probably true."

"It is. Oriel told Paul."

Randall nodded. They had arrived at the water's edge. Several groups of young children were playing on a long rectangle of grass, watched over by conscientious mothers and nannies.

Allison breathed deeply, enjoying the feel of the fresh air and the sun's rays on her face while a breeze playfully lifted her hair.

"Did he love her?" she asked after a moment.

"As a sister?" Randall asked. "Yes, I'm sure. As more than that? I don't know, but I have my suspicions."

"How did she die?"

"Oriel had problems for years. She was a victim of too much, too soon, I suppose. Too much responsibility, too much money. I'm sure it was hard for her. She started to drink, then she added pills. She shook the habit once, but just recently she must have slipped. She checked herself into one of those fix-it hospitals, and while she was there a wing of the place caught fire and she died along with three other patients. It was in all the papers."

"I rarely read a newspaper," Allison said.

"Why not?"

"I work."

"I work, too, but I generally find time for the *Chronicle*."

Allison didn't reply. She didn't want to get into the fact that her job at the restaurant wasn't her only one, or that the hours she had off from her jobs were spent caring for her grandfather. Instead her gaze followed the path of a sea gull as it landed on a piling, then busily spent its time there warning off other gulls.

Randall's gaze followed hers. He was silent for a moment, then he said, "Paul's driving you pretty hard, isn't he?"

Allison shrugged.

"Probably no harder than he's driving himself. He looked pretty awful just now."

"Does he ever smile?" Allison demanded impatiently. "I mean, really smile? Not that frigid pull of his lips that gives you the willies."

Randall smiled slightly. "Not often, not lately. Not since Oriel— Well, not since Oriel started to go downhill again. He was worried about her. He blames the people around her for her death. He thinks they encouraged her, aided her in her dependencies . . . that they helped force her back into the kind of life that made her check herself into that hospital in the first place."

"And did they?" Allison asked.

"They didn't help. Not from what Paul's told me."

"That first day. At the restaurant. He thought I was Oriel. He called me by her name—and he looked as if he'd seen a ghost."

Randall frowned. "He didn't tell me that."

Allison nodded. "He caused a scene. Armand had to escort him outside."

"Paul?" Randall questioned, shocked.

Allison nodded again. "The waitress I work with said he was crazy. And now here I am, working for him. But I don't think he's crazy. He's just—"

"—very determined," Randall supplied.

Allison grinned. She was feeling more like herself again—a fact she didn't want Paul Sullivan discovering—but it was something she badly needed, just as she'd needed to escape the intensity of the apartment, even if just for a few minutes.

Over the past week she'd eaten a little better, their meals having been delivered from a variety of nearby restaurants, and Paul Sullivan had watched her until satisfied that she'd eaten enough. And she had slept soundly, catching up on a great deal of much-needed rest. She didn't feel nearly as tired as she once had. Now if she could only manage to see her grandfather before she left the city, to assure herself that he was well. She also wanted to talk to his nurse, to be certain that she would be contacted if her grandfather encountered any problem. But she didn't know where she was going herself, and she doubted that Paul would tell her ahead of time since he wouldn't want her to receive any outside calls.

Suddenly she had an idea. She drew an excited breath and turned to the man at her side. "I wonder— Could I give your name and phone number to someone? Someone I might need to hear from at a moment's notice? You'd be able to get in touch with me, wouldn't you? To pass on a message?"

Randall merely stared at her. He didn't answer, he didn't look away. He had almost the same look as Paul had had that first day at the restaurant, one of stunned surprise.

"Randall?" Allison prompted. "What is it? I don't understand." In her confusion, her eyes lost some of their intense glow and her face lost its animation.

Randall shook himself free from bemusement. "Now, I'm beginning to understand Paul's problem," he murmured. "The poor sot's in even worse trouble than I thought. And he's probably not even aware of it himself yet."

"Does that mean that you won't do it?" she asked, clinging to her previous question. It was something she had to know.

Randall shook himself once again, trying to complete his reattachment. "Ah—no. Not at all. I don't mind. You can give my number to anyone you want."

"And do you know where we're going?" she probed.

"Some years ago Oriel's father built a big place on the Nevada side of Lake Tahoe. He used to have yearly house parties there for his followers. Oriel and Evan continued the practice."

Lake Tahoe! At least they weren't traveling halfway across the country as she'd begun to imagine. If her grandfather needed her, she could reach him fairly quickly by bus.

Randall stirred himself to look at his watch. "It's been almost an hour," he said. "I guess we'd better start back, before Paul thinks I've kidnapped you."

Allison paused to take another long look at the bay. She didn't want to return to the apartment yet. The freedom from pressure felt so wonderful. But at least she now had a better understanding of her employer. He had his troubles, just as she had hers. And just like her, he was trying to do something about them. Mutual need had brought them together, just as mutual need would undoubtedly see them through the worst of the upcoming weeks.

Without protest, she turned her back on the water and started across the street, Randall Peters walking smoothly at her side.

PAUL RETURNED to the apartment exactly forty-five minutes after having left it. When he read the note from Randall, he exploded. He had no right! He had asked him to *stay* with her, not accompany her wherever she wanted to go. To see the man she was so desperately intent upon seeing.

She had no right! He had given her his reason for keeping her isolated and she had thrown it back in his face. As usual. It always happened like that. Over and over again, he had to stand idly by and watch as she...

His thoughts jerked to a halt. Wait, he told himself. He wasn't dealing with Oriel. He wasn't having to stand helplessly by as she destroyed her life again. The woman he was teaching wasn't Oriel.

Paul reached blindly for the lamp atop his desk, twisted the switch, and was relieved to see the golden light that pooled in the corner of the room. Outside, night had not yet fallen, but in his soul it had. And he needed whatever forces he could muster to push the darkness away.

The sound of the outer door swinging shut caused him to snap upright.

Soon Randall stood in the archway, and by his side... Coming on the heels of his previous experience, Paul suffered another lapse. Breath was knocked completely from his lungs, his heart started to hammer thickly in his chest. Oriel was there again! *Oriel!* Then reality reasserted itself, leaving him trembling, shaken.

"Just what the hell did you think you were doing?" he demanded bitterly. "I told you I wanted her isolated! Not out doing God-knows-what with God-knows-who..."

"We took a short walk to the bay," Randall answered quietly, in direct contrast to his friend's agitation. "We met no one, talked to no one. She's as pristine now as she was when I came. Only she's a little more relaxed. Which is something you should try. Or have you forgotten how?"

"I haven't forgotten anything!" Paul snapped. "We only have a week... and as you, yourself, said, these people aren't fools."

"I remember saying a number of other things, as well."

Paul's gaze slid away from Randall's. His friend knew him too well, and he wasn't up to hiding his feelings. If he lapsed into silence, maybe Randall would take the unspoken message.

Randall must have done just that. He turned to Allison, and with his voice holding more warmth than Paul had heard him use in a long time, he said, "I very much enjoyed our walk. If you have a few minutes to spare at the end of next week let me know and we'll do it again."

Allison decided not to risk more trouble by answering. She merely smiled.

Randall turned back to Paul. "Allison and I will even let you come, if you want."

"Magda," Paul corrected tightly. "Her name is Magda."

Randall was silent for a moment, thinking, then he quoted, "*Revenge, at first thought sweet/ Bitter ere long back on itself recoils.* Milton, from *Paradise Lost*. I was just reading parts of it again last night. Seems appropriate, don't you think?"

"Am I going to have to throw you out?" Paul asked quietly, yet intently.

Randall heaved a short sigh, then as he was about to leave he lent an aside to Allison. "You have my phone number. Don't hesitate to call if you need me. And I won't forget what you asked, either."

Once Randall had gone Allison saw the building displeasure on Paul's face. Hoping to escape to her bedroom, she took several quick steps away.

"Wait! What did you ask him?" he demanded, stopping her.

Bravely she turned to meet his gaze. "Does it really matter?" she asked.

Their eyes locked for several long seconds. Battled silently. Then his were the first to break away.

Curiously she felt no elation.

Chapter Five

Allison's mind was populated by a wide variety of
people who kept shifting and changing, one into the
other. In comparison, learning Magda's history had
been simple. *These* people each had their own past
lives and their own motives, which were indelibly en-
twined with Oriel and her father and with each other.
Most had a spouse or a lover who seemed never to
leave their sides. It was like being thrust into the middle of a gigantic family quarrel and expected to know
everything about everyone within the first few minutes.

"No!" Paul snapped at the end of a very long day.
"Roger LeBlanc's wife is named Mary. Jennifer is
Jennifer Clark."

"Jim Clark's wife," Allison confirmed.

"Yes!"

"Jim Clark is the writer."

"Yes!"

"Roger LeBlanc is the film director. He also wrote
and produced *Spencer's Way*."

"Yes!"

Allison rubbed a throbbing temple. They had started the day early and had let up for no more than a few short minutes at lunch.

He pressed, "What about the others? What is Dusty Martin's wife's name?"

"Dusty Martin isn't married. But the woman he's been living with for the past five years is Jean Anne Shafer. She's his collaborator. They've written several commercial jingles that were fairly successful. But nothing recently." She paused, then breaking away from rote, said, "I remember Dusty Martin now! He had a variety show on TV when I was a child."

"He had his fifteen minutes of fame," Paul acknowledged.

"My Dad was a big fan of his."

"What about Frank Alexander?" he immediately questioned.

"I don't remember him."

Paul seemed barely able to control his impatience. "I'm not asking if you recall him from childhood. I'm asking if you remember him now."

Emotionally Allison curled back into herself. For a moment she had felt like a human being, not merely a tape recorder that could be rewound and played back at will. Each day of this week had been worse than the one before. If the weekend ever did come, would he even know that *she* existed? He had formed her in a pattern of his own making, but somewhere along the way he had forgotten that she had a soul.

"Frank Alexander is a playwright that Damien—our father—promised to back, but never did. The promise is to be kept through his will, though, on stipulation that his heir not object. Oriel had cause to object. I might or I might not."

Paul Sullivan rose from his chair to walk to the fireplace mantel, where he fingered a small brass dog. "Oriel objected because Alexander is a fool. He wouldn't know talent if it jumped up and bit him. He made Oriel's life miserable with his continual begging. What was she supposed to do? Hand over the money just to make him go away? If she did, he'd be back in three months wanting more."

Nothing was ever Oriel's fault. At least not to Paul. The woman had been a saint, to his way of thinking. She had wanted only to help the people who surrounded her, but had been prevented from doing so by the myriad complications of her father's will.

"He's not married," she continued her spiel. "He's had one failed marriage and doesn't seem to be contemplating another."

"He's also an alcoholic!"

Allison was sympathetic. Her father hadn't been an alcoholic, but frequently he had used liquor as a crutch. "He must be very unhappy," she said, thinking of her father.

Paul's head whipped around. "We're in business to make them even more unhappy. Now tell me what you know of Oriel's husband."

Allison rubbed her temple again. Sometimes all she wanted to do was scream at him, tell him to stop—she had absorbed all that she possibly could! But whenever she was tempted to protest, she thought of the steadier financial position she and her grandfather would be in at the end of these few weeks. A few weeks... What was a few weeks?

"Evan Sargent was Oriel's third husband," she repeated. "They'd been married for ten years when she died. They had no children. Evan is a gambler and a schemer, and Oriel backed any number of his failed ventures along the way. He had a little money of his own when they married, but he's been living off her for years. It's rumored that he's..."

"...NEAR BANKRUPTCY. He denies it, but it's common knowledge. He pretended to be devoted to Oriel, when everyone knew that he had a mistress on the side. Even Oriel knew." Allison paused, smoothing one icy hand over the other.

They were almost there. Paul had kept her repeating backgrounds from the instant they left the tiny airfield nestled in the mountains. Since he had produced photographs for her to study several days before, her attempts to keep everyone straight had become much simpler. She could now parrot information as if she had known it all her life. She understood how one person related to another and how she, as Magda, related to each of them. Of himself and his

position, Paul said nothing. But in saying nothing—
this time—he had told her a great deal.

Paul split his concentration between what she was
saying and the twisting road ahead. He didn't seem to
notice the deep blue beauty of Lake Tahoe, set like a
jewel in a ring of mountains, or the touches of spring
snow that still clung to the higher elevations of the
Sierra range.

"All right," he said at last, frowning. "I suppose
you have it. Now all you have to do is try not to sound
as if everything's memorized."

"I can do that," she claimed. "I can!" she said
again, when she thought she saw doubt flicker in his
quick glance. After all the work she had done over the
past two weeks, she wasn't going to allow him to un-
dermine what little confidence she had managed to
gather. Especially when they were within a few
hundred yards of their destination. "If you're having
second thoughts," she warned, "just stop the car right
now and let me out. Let me go back to San Francisco! This wasn't my idea in the first place, remember? You were the one who insisted. You were the one
who wanted me to do it. Just stop the car! *Stop it!*"
she cried, hurt pride having turned into panic. Could
she do it? Would she be able to convince *anyone?* She
wasn't a professional actress! Whatever had made him
think... Made *her* think...?

"What I don't need now is an hysteric!" he snapped
with ice-like calm. "I'm not stopping this car and
you're not getting out. The two of us have an ar-

rangement and we're going to see it through. You're not going to pull out on me at the last second."

"I can refuse to participate," she claimed.

"Like hell you can!" He settled the dispute by increasing the car's speed.

Allison shot him a resentful glance. His handsome features looked carved from stone, and his heart was just as hard. He had one obsession in his life and that was avenging Oriel. No matter what it took, no matter who got hurt!

His ruthlessness caused her to shudder. To him, she was merely a tool. He had never asked her a thing about herself. She had no history, and as far as he was concerned, no future. Only the present counted, because of the use he planned to make of it...and of her.

THE HOUSE CLINGING to the side of a hill could more easily be termed a mansion. Positioned at the edge of a grove of tall pines, it took up more space than three normal houses. Boasting wide landscaped terraces, a covered swimming pool and several tennis courts, it still managed to blend in with its rustic surroundings. Built of what looked to be rough cedar, a series of elongated windows took prime advantage of the spectacular view of the mountains and lake.

Allison took an unsteady breath as the car drew to a stop along the wide driveway. Paul turned to look at her. She felt the sweep of his dark gaze as it moved over the white silk dress that had been chosen with special care from the wardrobe he had purchased for her. He was going for a certain look, he had told her. Innocent yet with a budding sophistication, a dress that would be a subtle threat. Also under his direction, she had learned to apply her makeup as he desired. A touch of mascara and eye pencil, a light blush, a lip gloss more than an actual stain. All else was left to her natural coloring. Her hair had been pulled loosely back from her face and held at the crown by a clasp. He had even chosen the perfume she was wearing. Oriel's favorite, he murmured when he gave it to her.

Allison swallowed. She was so nervous, so afraid. If only he would give her the smallest measure of encouragement...

"You look perfect," he said, as if somehow aware of her need. "They're not going to know what hit them."

Allison looked away. With one hand he had offered relief. With the other, he had destroyed it. The responsibility to cause such a shock was overwhelming.

He came round to open her door, and when she straightened at his side, he presented his arm. Allison hesitated before taking it. She had never touched him before. Not in all the time they had been together. Neither had he touched her. Never a hint of physical contact had been initiated between them. Quite the opposite, in fact. Therefore, touching him now made her feel awkward, adding to her uncertainty.

She glanced at his austere profile as they walked side by side toward the house. If he even noticed their contact, it would surprise her. *He* was the one like a machine, she decided. Clipping out orders and directives and playing the stern taskmaster, never once letting down, never once showing a human side.

Allison was aware of the fine quivering that had taken hold of her body. Could she do it? Could she convince them?

THEIR ARRIVAL WAS TIMED perfectly to interrupt the evening meal. Paul had wanted everyone together and this was the only time he could be sure that they would all be gathered in the same room. As they made their way through the house, Allison absorbed as much as she could of its decor. The interior was just as breathtaking as the exterior, if not more so. Each room was wide and open, with high ceilings dusted at the wall tops with either moldings or stencilings or both, while green plants—large and small—calmed the eye and gave accent to individual furnishings. The floors were constructed of pale hardwood over which, at periodic intervals, were spread thick, rich rugs.

Laughter coming from the dining room caused Paul's mouth to immediately tighten.

He motioned for Allison to wait. Then, without making a sound, he stepped around the corner into the room.

Laughter continued for another moment, then stopped suddenly.

"What the—" someone breathed, startled.

"You!" someone else exclaimed.

Several other voices rose, echoing surprise.

She could hear the dry mockery in Paul's tone as he inquired smoothly, "I was invited, wasn't I?"

Voices fell one over the other until a strong masculine baritone took precedence. "Of course you were invited. We just didn't expect you, that's all. Not after what you said at the memorial . . ."

"I've brought a guest," Paul interrupted. The coldness of his disdain was daunting, even to Allison.

There was a brief pause. "That's allowed," the man replied. "But where—?"

Paul stepped back and directed Allison to come to him.

Allison hesitated. This was the moment she had dreaded. His eyes, meeting hers, glittered with anticipation. Allison drew a breath and stepped to his side.

If Paul's appearance had startled everyone, her presence flabbergasted them. Shocked gasps escaped from faces drained of color. Those who had stood to confront Paul collapsed into their chairs.

Paul's smile was malicious. "Ladies and gentlemen—and I use those terms loosely—I'd like to introduce someone who has a special place in all of our hearts—Magda Richards. You remember that name, don't you? Oriel's sister? The person you never expected to meet? Not in a thousand years . . . but especially not now!"

More gasps. A reflexive cry. It was all Allison could do to look at them. She hated being the agent of such chagrin, whether dealing with truth or not. But strangely, she couldn't force her gaze away. Her eyes moved over each of them who, even in their shock, she found easy to identify:

At the head of the table sat Evan Sargent, looking exactly like his picture—tall and thin, with smoothly styled gray hair, he exuded a dapper confidence that came only as a result of intimate acquaintance with the finer things in life.

To his left sat Jennifer Clark, still looking like the glamorous model she had been some fifteen years before. With her mane of thick blond hair and beautifully structured features, only the march of time had pushed her from her place before the still cameras. Next to her was her husband, Jim, rather nondescript, with fading blond hair and the restless eyes of a man who was constantly nettled by his wife's discontent.

Next to him was Frank Alexander, whom Paul had described as an excessive drinker. At the moment, though, he merely looked a fairly harmless middle-aged man with a neatly trimmed mustache and thinning medium brown hair.

Roger LeBlanc claimed the seat at the far end of the table. At first glance his air of tough intelligence seemed at odds with the insipid blankness of his wife, but a closer look at Mary, seated to his left, revealed a much harder edge.

Allison recognized Dusty Martin instantly, and would have done so without the help of a photograph. With his familiar shock of orange-red hair and his multitude of freckles, true flamboyance enlivened his face to belie his fifty-three years.

Completing the table was Dusty's current lover, Jean Anne Shafer, who seemed to share his need to challenge conventionality. Her jet black hair was cut short and stood on end, which echoed her heavy makeup and odd manner of dress.

"Smile," Paul hissed in Allison's ear, jerking her away from her thoughts.

She did the best she could, managing a shy, self-conscious pull of her lips, which disappeared almost as quickly as it appeared.

Evan Sargent choked, "Paul, if this is your idea of a joke—"

"Oh, this is no joke," Paul assured. "Would I do something like that to you? To any of you? When you all were so close to Oriel? And behaved so caringly?"

"See here, Paul!" Dusty Martin sputtered.

Paul switched his gaze to the man whose many freckles now stood out like flags on his pasty white skin. "Yes, Dusty? You have something to say? In defense, perhaps?"

"Where did you find her, Paul?" Jennifer Clark asked. She was the first to recover her wits enough to offer a coherent challenge.

Paul chided, "Aren't any of you going to say hello? Where are your manners?"

Several heads turned toward Evan. Since he was the host, the pressure was on him.

Evan blustered, "You can't just walk in here as if nothing has happened, and demand..."

"Oh, something's happened, all right. Oriel's dead! Even though none of you seems to care."

"We *know* she's dead! We don't need you to tell us that!" Evan defended. "I, above all people..."

"You, above all people, should be mourning her loss! Not having a party to celebrate!"

"This is what she'd want, Paul. We're not doing anything that she wouldn't approve. If she were here, she'd tell you herself."

"But she's not here, is she Evan? And that's what the whole matter comes down to. She's *not* here, and she won't ever be here again! And that makes all of you extremely happy! Except for one very small matter—" Paul thrust Allison to the forefront like a prize "—Magda!"

"I don't believe this!" Roger LeBlanc swore coldly, his hands clenching into fists on the edge of the table.

"Believe it," Paul said. "Take a good look. How could she possibly be anyone else?"

Allison felt the weight of eight pairs of eyes. She tried to control the trembling of her limbs, hoping that no one would notice.

"I asked a question," Jennifer Clark insisted. "Where did you find her?"

"Do you think I just picked her up off the street? *Look at her!*"

Again eight pairs of eyes concentrated on Allison. They probed her face, her form.

"She's thinner than Oriel," Jean Anne Shafer complained.

"I never said she was Oriel."

"How old is she?" Jim Clark asked, following his wife's lead in initiating the expected quiz.

"Ask her," Paul deferred.

"How old are you?" Jim Clark repeated.

Allison glanced quickly at Paul. He gave her no encouragement; he merely stood there, waiting, like all the rest. She cleared her throat nervously. "Twenty-two."

"Where do you come from?"

"What proof do you have that you are who you say you are?"

"Why are you doing this . . . for the money?"

The hostile questions crashed against her.

Paul intervened. He drew Allison back under the protection of his arm and raised a hand to quiet them. "She can't answer all of you at once! If you can't be civil, you can wait. Right now Magda's tired and needs rest. She's had a long journey."

"Can't she say that for herself?" Jennifer Clark murmured dryly.

Paul ignored the remark. "Evan, I'm taking her to Oriel's suite. And I'll use my usual room down the hall. You don't object, do you?"

"Do I have a choice?" Evan asked. "But I still want to see your proof!"

Paul's smile signaled utter confidence. "Oh, we have proof, all right. Do you think I'd bring an impostor here? I'd be a fool."

"I wouldn't put anything past you, Paul," Frank Alexander said, coming into the conversation for the first time.

"The feeling is mutual, Frank."

The two men glared at one another until Allison moved uncomfortably beneath Paul's arm. He broke his gaze away to look at her. For the space of a second, Allison thought she saw something flash in his eyes, then it was gone and he was speaking to her formally, "Magda, I apologize for everyone's bad behavior. But I did warn you that your arrival would be something of a shock. Possibly everyone will have collected themselves by the time we meet again, and they'll be in a much more hospitable mood."

"I still want to see your proof!" Evan insisted.

Paul had started for the door, bringing Allison with him. He stopped, turning. "Evan, I wonder if Mrs. Wainwright could be persuaded to bring our dinner to Oriel's suite. We wouldn't dream of disrupting your meal any further."

"You bastard," Jennifer said tightly.

"Certainly," Evan replied.

Paul started away again.

Allison went with him, looking neither right nor left. She was afraid of what she might see. From the animosity they had created in that room, a knife whizzing past wouldn't have surprised her in the least.

THE SECOND-FLOOR SUITE Paul showed her to was just as magnificent as the rest of the house, if not more so. Like something from a dream, it was dominated by cream-colored satins and laces. Every jar, every bowl, every figurine was crafted lovingly enough to take one's breath away. A giant wardrobe painted in white gloss took up most of the length of one wall, while a huge four-poster bed made of some kind of dark hardwood was piled high with additional mounds of cream satin and lace. A sofa covered in a soft golden fabric was placed comfortably in the sitting area along with a small round table and lamp.

Allison stared, wide-eyed, at the evidence of such opulence. She had never *seen* such a glorious set of rooms before, much less contemplated living in them.

"I can't stay here!" she exclaimed. "It's so...so..."

"What's wrong with it?" Paul asked suspiciously, frowning as he looked around.

"...wonderful!" she completed, perfectly serious.

Allison was aware of Paul's surging satisfaction at the chaos they had left behind in the dining room. He was extremely pleased with the way things had turned out and he gave the first genuine laugh that she had ever heard him use.

"Oh, you'll stay here all right. As Magda, this is where you belong. It will help establish your identity. You did very well downstairs. They're thrown totally off balance."

"I don't feel as if I did anything at all. I only answered one question."

"You established exactly the feel I was looking for. Innocent and yet— And it looked very real. Quite a good acting job. Keep it up and I might even be persuaded to give you a bonus! That should make you happy."

Allison didn't know what to say. She hadn't been acting!

"My room is the first door on the right down the hall," he continued. "Oriel liked to have me nearby, even if she never—" Again his words stopped. "When the meal comes, eat it. You're probably going to need every bit of strength you can muster."

Allison looked at him. "What about you? Aren't you going to eat, too?"

He shook his head. "I'm not hungry."

Neither was she. But she withheld comment. She had been given her instructions. What she felt about the matter didn't concern him.

Allison watched as he strode confidently to the door. Tall and leanly muscled, his carefully chosen clothing fitted him perfectly. In all the time she had known him—was it just two weeks?—he had never let down. Not for him a wardrobe of jeans and T-shirts and a comfortable sweater. But he looked right in what he wore, handsome. Like a dark knight in one of the fairy tales her mother used to read to her. The knight with a terrible secret hurt hidden in his past. He never won the girl, of course; that was left to the knight whose armor shone. Yet it was always the dark knight who had fascinated her so much more.

Allison jerked her gaze away from him, shocked and surprised by her sudden thought. Flights of fancy had no place in this situation. What was to take place in this house was serious business. And she, normally serious, had better keep it that way.

Chapter Six

Everything was progressing exactly as Paul had planned. Blood had literally drained from their faces when she stepped into the room! One or two had even looked near to passing out! Their pitiful bravado was merely a cover for their fear.

She was perfect. Perfect in the way she looked, in the way she moved, in the shy innocence that she projected. It might all be an act, but it was wonderful. Wonderful!

But if everything was so damned wonderful, why did he have this nagging feeling of unease?

He should be on top of the world right now, ready to reap the fruits of his hard labor.

No one who looked at the situation objectively would blame him! He was doing what had to be done. Repaying a debt he owed Oriel. Repaying them for betraying her, betraying her trust. He didn't give a damn what Randall said. Randall was wrong.

Still he felt this...uneasiness. He began to pace the bedroom floor, trying to figure it out.

It had to be his return to this house. A return to even stronger memories of Oriel. She was everywhere here, in every room, looking at him with those jewel-like eyes. With reproach? Why reproach? Because he hadn't been there when she needed him most? Because he had been in bed, asleep, when the fire had...

Paul groaned. He couldn't think that way! He couldn't hold himself responsible for that. He didn't know that she had checked into the institute. Even if he had, he couldn't have prevented...

Still, it didn't stop him from feeling guilty. Just as he had felt guilty that he was safe in a hotel when his parents died on that mountaintop in Austria.

He ran a hand through his hair. He knew that wasn't logical. Neither accident had been his fault; he couldn't have prevented either. Still...

He was surprised to see that his hand was trembling. Was the pressure too much? Was he beginning to crack up? Had the process that started that fateful day at the restaurant degenerated to the point of dementia?

His thoughts went back to the moment in his apartment when he had confused *her* for Oriel. It had happened before, of course, but that had been when he was in shock. The second time, there had been no excuse. Not really. He had tried to blame it on stress then, but what about the third time...and the fourth? Momentary flashes that he'd been unable to discount.

A light sweat broke over his body; his heart began a rapid tattoo.

He had to *do* something! He had to stop *thinking*! Otherwise...

Paul veered into the attached bath and as he went he peeled off his clothing. By the time he stood in front of the mirrored shower door he was naked.

Naked to everything but himself?

The unwanted thought would not be denied, neither would its companion.

Was it because he was afraid of what he might see?

For a terrible moment Paul was afraid to look in the mirror. When finally he did, he saw that nothing had changed... at least, not on the outside.

THERE WAS NO HINT of the uncertainty that was beginning to plague Paul's spirit as he escorted his protégée into the lion's den. To those assembled, he looked maddeningly assured.

His gaze swept their faces. Their hostility had not abated; neither had their fear. He smiled.

"All right," he said. "Let's begin."

He had felt the tension in Allison's body as she walked down the stairs at his side, but he hadn't taken the time to talk to her. They both knew what was to come; they were both prepared.

Evan Sargent stood up. The library was a massive area used more for social occasions than for reading. Books lined the walls, but Damien Woodrich had chosen them for looks rather than information. Nei-

ther Oriel nor Evan had added to the collection.
Couches and chairs of soft leather were spotted about
the room, most concentrating around a flagstone
fireplace over which the trophy head of a giant ram
glared defiantly at those gathered below.

"Yes. I'm ready to begin," Evan said. He walked
over to Allison and examined her with narrowed eyes.
He then moved in a circle around her, pushing Paul
out of the way when he needed past, an act that
wordlessly underlined his disdain. When he had completed a full circuit, he demanded, "My wife tried for
years to find you. Why have you come now?"

Instinctively Allison disliked Evan Sargent. Not
because of anything Paul had told her, since she wasn't
sure exactly how much she could rely on his judgment
in regard to these people, but because he reminded her
of that small minority of people who came into the
restaurant and the bookstore and expected to be ca-
tered to like royalty. Rudeness to those forced to wait
upon them was commonplace. Her chin tilted a small
degree even as she remembered her role and kept her
voice soft. "Oriel and I exchanged letters recently. She
knew where I was."

"Why didn't she say anything to me?" he demanded.

"Because she wanted to keep my location a secret."

"Oh, my...how convenient!" The voice of a
woman intervened. Allison glanced toward Mary
LeBlanc, then back at Evan.

"And where was that?" Evan continued.

Allison felt the malevolence of his gaze, of all their gazes. "I'd rather not say."

Roger LeBlanc shot to his feet. "Oh, come on, now! You can't expect us to swallow that!" He was a large man with a hard face and a jutting nose that dominated his features. "Why, if I tried that with a producer, he'd throw me straight out of his office. Tell us the truth or get out of here, Paul."

Paul didn't look the least upset. "Give her a chance, Roger. Don't jump down her throat first thing."

"She's *had* a chance and she's..."

"Marabu," Allison inserted. "It's a small island off..."

"We all know where it is!" Evan snapped. "I even went there once with Oriel, when she was determined to find you. But we came away with nothing. Nothing! And it's not that big a place. You can practically walk across it in three hours! Try again, Miss Whatever-your-name-is. You're not doing very well."

Paul reached into his jacket pocket and extracted an envelope. "Maybe you'd better take a look at this, Evan. Before you make a complete fool of yourself."

Evan snatched the envelope from Paul's fingers and unfolded the letter inside. He read the contents with disbelief. "A convent? You expect me to believe she grew up in a *convent!*"

"Why not? When it's true." Paul smiled, enjoying Evan's perplexity. "Do you see the signature and the seal on the bottom of the page?"

Evan blustered, his face growing pink. "Anyone can fake a seal . . . and a signature! And just who the hell is this Sister Dominica? I don't believe this! I don't believe it for one minute!"

Jennifer Clark reached for the paper. She read it before passing it to the others.

"You'll have to do better than that, Paul," she drawled, but there was an edge to her words.

Paul produced another paper. "How about a birth certificate?" He handed it to Evan. "And a letter from Oriel to Magda."

Evan examined those papers, too. Again they were whisked away by Jennifer as soon as he was through.

"That was my last letter from Oriel," Allison said. "When I read about the fire, I contacted Paul."

"Why Paul?" Roger demanded.

Allison returned his look levelly. "Because Oriel told me to . . . if anything ever happened to her."

Her answer set off numerous protests. She and Paul weathered them without comment.

"It's just too convenient!" Dusty Martin burst out. "Too damned convenient! Especially now, when—" Jean Anne, sitting on the arm of Dusty's chair, reached out to silence him. The redhead's words drew to an immediate halt.

"Yes, isn't it?" Paul gloated. "When all of you expected to get your way at last. But it isn't going to work out like that, is it? Too bad."

"This isn't any of your business, Paul!" Frank Alexander spoke up. "It never has been. Our relationship with Oriel and her father doesn't concern you in the least. You're not in Damien's will."

Paul's body stiffened. He wanted to physically attack the man. "Unlike the rest of you," he said coldly. "My concern has never been money."

"Oriel was bored with you," Jennifer Clark said nastily. "She told me so."

"Only after she listened to your lies! You have a lot to answer for, Jennifer."

Jennifer pulled a defiant face.

Evan broke into the argument. "That's enough! We're not here to go over old ground. You said your piece at the memorial service, Paul. We all know how you feel. You've made your contempt for us perfectly clear over the years. What we need to decide at this moment is the veracity of this young woman's story, and I, for one, am not satisfied!"

"I'm sure you're not," Paul murmured, his hatred for the man evident in his eyes.

"I'm going to have the story checked . . ."

"I was sure you would."

"Damn you, Paul! Let me speak!"

Paul gave a mock bow.

Evan drew into what he must have thought was a posture of authority, but the effect was merely pompous. "We wish to speak to her alone. We don't want you interrupting."

"I won't say another word."

"Are you afraid to leave her alone with us? Afraid we'll discover the truth?"

Paul glanced at his protégée. She returned his look without expression. "Talk to her as long as you wish," he dismissed. "I'm not worried."

Evan walked to the door and held it open. "Then you won't mind leaving us?"

Paul's expression never changed as he stepped into the hall. "I'll be on the front terrace," he said. "If one of you would be kind enough to show Magda the way."

"Of course," Evan said formally.

ALLISON WATCHED PAUL GO. She wanted to cry out, to beg him to take her with him! But he was gone from the room before she could utter a word.

She turned to look at the assembly. Their hostility was now tinged with anticipation as their focus turned solely to her. They were waiting to tear her apart.

Evan Sargent resumed the seat he had claimed before their arrival. He did not offer her the courtesy of a chair.

"So," he began, "you claim to be Magda Richards. Would you like to give us one good reason why we should believe you? Apart from your resemblance to Oriel, which, I admit, is uncanny. But looks can be altered. It's not that difficult."

"You have the papers..." she began.

"Papers can be forged. You must forgive us, but we have a lot at stake here. Please answer the question."

Allison's gaze moved from one person to another. Some answering gazes were stonier than others, but all were united in their desire to discredit her.

"All I have is the truth," she said simply.

"And that is?"

Allison hated to lie. It went against every scruple inside her. But she was playing a part, carrying a role. She had known it would come to this from the beginning. "I *am* Magda Richards."

"What was your father's name?" Jennifer Clark asked.

"Damien Woodrich."

"And your mother?"

"My mother was Amelia Richards."

"What was Oriel to you?"

"My half sister."

"Why did you live apart?"

"My mother brought me to Marabu when I was an infant . . . to escape from my father."

"Why?" Mary LeBlanc demanded.

"I was illegitimate, but he wanted me. My mother was afraid he would take me away from her."

"What happened to your mother?" Frank Alexander asked.

"She died. When I was fifteen."

"Why didn't you come back here then? Your father was still alive. He'd have welcomed you with open arms."

"I was afraid of him, too. My mother... When my mother knew she was going to die, she arranged with the sisters to protect me."

"How quaint," Jennifer mocked.

Frank threw the woman an irritated look, but he said nothing.

Dusty took up the cause. He motioned irritably. "I could care less about what happened in the past. What I want to know is—if you are who you say you are, what are you going to do now? Where do we fit into your plans?"

"Don't be stupid, Dusty!" Mary LeBlanc rebuked. "If we can prove she's not Magda, we won't have to worry!"

Dusty returned the rebuke. "You want to tell me just how we're going to do that?"

"We make her prove it."

"She already has!" He waved the paper from the convent. "This looks pretty authentic to me!"

There were more protests.

Evan retook command. "That's enough!" he said gruffly. "We're not doing ourselves any good by fighting." He turned back to Allison. In his hand was the letter Paul had produced only that morning and which, in actuality, had been written by Oriel. Only Paul had discarded the first page, where the salutation was to him and dated some years before. The contents of the letter fitted this situation perfectly. Oriel had been concerned about her first episode of dependency but had tried to assure him that all would turn out well. It could easily have been written in the past few months.

Evan lifted the page, reread it, then lowering it asked, "Where's the first page?"

"I destroyed it."

"For what reason?"

"It contained something personal."

"As if this doesn't?"

Oriel's words had rambled, but they had also been an aching plea for understanding. Allison's heart had wrenched upon reading them.

"It was something personal between Oriel and myself. I didn't want anyone else to read it."

"What did she tell you? Was it something about one of us?"

Allison frowned. She hadn't expected such a question. "No. As I said, it was personal."

"How did you learn of her death?"

"The newspaper."

"There are newspapers in convents?" Jim Clark asked, a muscle twitching at the side of his jaw.

"Of course."

"Are you a nun?" Jean Anne Shafer asked curiously.

Jennifer smirked, gaining a spiteful look from Jean Anne.

"No," Allison answered. "I'm not . . . not yet."

There was an immediate focusing of attention. All eyes bored into her.

"You mean . . . you might . . . become one?" Jean Anne was left to ask the question that each was thinking.

Allison called upon all her powers of persuasion. This was where she really started to act. Her answer needed to be subtle, extending the possibility yet at the same time taking it away.

"I might," she said.

Her answer stunned them, left them unsure. She had succeeded.

Evan cleared his throat. "This . . . Sister Dominica. Is she available for us to speak to?"

Allison shook her head. "I'm afraid not. The entire convent is on retreat. She will speak to no one for the next two weeks unless it's an emergency."

"But this *is* an emergency!" Dusty wailed.

Resistance was beginning to crumble. They were starting to believe her! Allison could sense the shift.

She decided to seize her advantage. "May I go now? This *has* been a very long day. Three different flights. If we could talk again tomorrow?"

Evan's complexion had grayed. "Yes, of course," he agreed, but his mind wasn't totally involved with what he was saying as he grappled with the complexities of what he had learned.

Frank Alexander stood up. "I'll take you to Paul," he volunteered.

No one tried to stop them as they left the room. Just as Evan was busy trying to understand the precariousness of his newfound position, so were the others grappling with the idea that they, too, might be forced to play under yet another new set of rules.

ALLISON FELT FRANK Alexander's curious glance as they moved down the hall toward the front of the house.

"You've really set the fox among the chickens," he commented softly. "My question is—who's the fox? I suspect the culprit is Paul."

"I don't know what you mean," she denied, knowing full well what he meant.

The playwright's face was lined with many fine wrinkles, and when he smiled the ones at the corners of his eyes fanned into the graying brown hair at his temples. They were the best signal of his humor because his mustache disguised the pull of his lips.

"I've been around actresses most of my life," he explained. "I'm accustomed to putting words in their mouths...or at least attempting to. I can't honestly say that I've been very successful in this endeavor, but I know a good performance when I see one. Don't worry, though, I won't give you away. I think it will be much too much fun to watch."

"I still don't..."

"Don't worry about Roger, either. He's so far removed from directing that he's forgotten everything he learned. He's only interested in money now. How much he can get, and how easily. Oh, he was good once. One of the best around. *Spencer's Way* wasn't a fluke. But he's gotten lazy."

"Mr. Alexander!" Allison cried. "Please. I . . ."

"Call me Frank. It'll drive Paul up the wall."

They had arrived at the set of French doors that led from the forepart of the house to the front terrace.

Frank Alexander opened one of the doors and gallantly motioned for Allison to precede him.

Paul, who had been pacing across the brick patio, halted when they stepped outside. He frowned as he noted Allison's heightened color and Frank's general air of amusement.

"I'm delivering Magda, as promised," Frank said. "I'm probably the safest of them all. I don't bite."

"Don't believe him, Magda," Paul directed tightly.

Allison moved instinctively closer to Paul, which caused Frank's eye creases to deepen. "If it's worth anything, I salute your effort, Paul. You made a good choice when you picked her. But then with the way she looks, it would be hard to choose anyone else. By God, she could easily *be* Oriel!"

"There's a good reason for that," Paul said stiffly. "It's called genes."

"Ah—but you don't say *whose* genes she inherited."

Frank continued to smile as he gave a little bow, then returned to the house through the door they had exited.

Paul glanced sharply at Allison and said, "We're going for a walk."

His declaration was totally unexpected. "A walk?" she repeated.

"Away from the house."

Immediately Allison understood. She fell into place at his side.

They came upon a well-kept trail that led through the trees at the side of the house. Enough light remained from the lowering sun to illuminate the pathway ahead. The sloping descent was gradual.

At first Paul said nothing, then he asked, "Was it difficult?"

"It wasn't easy."

"Did they believe you?"

"I think so."

"What about Frank?"

She shrugged. "I'm not sure."

"Be careful of him. He's not as harmless as he looks. Especially when he's had too much to drink, which is usually the case."

"He seemed all right today."

"Just be careful...be careful of all of them. They're not above trying to get on your good side while planning all the while to stab you in the back."

"If they're all so untrustworthy," Allison mused curiously, "why did Oriel put up with them? Why didn't she just ask them to leave? She could have, couldn't she? I mean...it was within her power."

Her words trailed away, when she realized that she had overstepped the bounds he had set up between them. The dark expression that seemed so much a part of his makeup returned again in force. He didn't like her talking about Oriel, especially if what she had to say could in any way be deemed derogatory.

With stiff formality, he said, "I want to give them time to think. When we get back to the house, go straight to your room and stay there. They shouldn't see you again tonight."

Then he turned around and their return to the house was completed in silence.

ALLISON WAS RELIEVED to escape from everyone's surveillance.

Today had been much more difficult than she had thought and tomorrow would probably be worse. Her original worry was that she wouldn't be able to convince them; her worry now was that she had.

The situation reminded her of her grandfather's story of the little girl who tried for hours to get a sleepy lion to follow her... and didn't know what to do with him when he did. Well, the lion was now following *her!*

Exactly what responsibility did she bear in all of this? Could she excuse herself because she was being paid? Was that good enough, when she saw how many lives she was disrupting? Even if they were lives, from Paul's witness, that were not without great yawning faults? But whose life didn't have faults?

She wished she could speak for just a short time with her grandfather... speak with him as she once had, when he would give her the wise counsel of his accumulated years. Would he have understood what she was doing? Would he have advised her against it? Probably. Her grandfather had always been a scrupulously honest man.

Allison curled up in one corner of the beautiful golden sofa and, emotionally exhausted, closed her eyes. She could not yet bring herself to intrude upon the bed.

Chapter Seven

Allison awoke the next morning in much the same position as she had fallen asleep. The bed, with its fluffy pillows and inviting satin-and-lace comforter, remained untouched. When first she moved her muscles ached, especially the muscles of her neck. But after sitting up and stretching, most of the stiffness disappeared.

She remembered nothing after her attack of conscience the previous night, except for a deep case of self-pity, which was something the light of a new day very effectively dispelled. As long as she had strength and ability, she could work her way through any difficulty. She shouldn't be concerned, she told herself. She was here to do a job. That was all. It would be foolish of her to even consider backing out now. She bore no responsibility to these people. She didn't even know them! Paul did, and it was he who wanted revenge. She was merely his instrument—as he, no doubt, thought of her.

Allison stretched again and let her gaze make another sweep of the interior of the room. Her opinion did not change from yesterday. It was absolutely beautiful. If the decor of a room mirrored the personality of its owner, Oriel had been very feminine, had known exactly what she liked and had not been afraid to demand it.

Which was at odds with the wrenching words of turmoil that had filled the pages of her letter.

Two different Oriels seemed to exist in the same person. Paul had seen a saint; had the others seen someone different?

Allison moved away from the couch, trailing around the perimeter of the room. She stopped to examine more closely the jars and bowls and figurines, the silver- and porcelain-framed pictures of people she didn't recognize—until she found one of Paul. A much younger Paul, barely in his twenties. Extremely handsome, even then, with his dark hair and eyes and just an edge of melancholy.

At the wardrobe she paused at the tall doors and pulled them open. Inside, it was full of clothing— dresses and blouses, skirts and jackets. Along the center was a line of drawers and in them lay some of the most beautiful lingerie Allison had ever seen. All in hues that went perfectly with Oriel's coloring and therefore her own.

Allison touched them reverently. She had never seen so much opulence outside a store. To think that someone actually had *owned* all these things!

Shoes lined the bottom of the wardrobe. Innumerable pairs. Allison couldn't help herself; she slipped her foot into one of the leather pumps and marveled that their feet had been exactly the same size.

Had they worn the same dress size as well? Was it possible?

Quickly she closed both doors. No. She wasn't here to snoop. She had her own clothes—the ones that Paul had bought for Magda—which were still in the suitcase, she belatedly realized. After her shower, she would hang them up and possibly see if she could find an iron or a steamer.

Allison escaped into the bathroom. She didn't see how anyone could ever get used to living in this manner. The richness of marble, the gold-plated faucets and handles...

There was no shower, so Allison climbed the three steps to the tub—but this was no mere tub. It was more like a small swimming pool! She turned a tap, waited for the water to heat, then mixed cool with it until the temperature was perfect. As the tub filled she slowly undressed, inhibited by her reflection in the set of mirrors that backed it. Cast with a warm bronze tint, they turned her body into a living statue, burnished as if by the sun, and her hair into ribbons of glowing flame.

Allison caught her breath. She could barely believe that it was herself she saw in the mirror. Surely it was Oriel come back to life to reclaim her place and her property.

She lifted a tentative hand to her mouth, touched it and watched as the reflection echoed the movement. Thankfully the warmth of her finger against her lips helped to anchor her and break the spell.

The reality of the water also aided in her return to herself. She was Allison. Allison Williams. She repeated her name over and over as she slowly submerged her hips. Still, for a moment she trembled.

Her bath was accomplished quickly. Then wrapping a huge soft towel about her body, she went in search of her suitcase. It wasn't where she had last seen it. She continued the search and finally found it tucked away in a closet to one side of the bedroom. It was there that she also found her clothing, hanging neatly on a closet rod, with no wrinkles or upturned collars in the group. The housekeeper, or one of her helpers, must have performed the service while Allison was absent, coming and going without notice. Quietly performing her duties.

Allison knew she would never become accustomed to such an idea. She could never accept the ministrations of a maid, possibly because she felt that she was too close to being one herself. A waitress and a salesclerk were near the same thing. All performed a service. One to a private few; the others to the public.

Allison dressed as rapidly as she could, feeling a growing need to get out of this room!

She was at the door, ready to open it, when a tap sounded from the other side.

PAUL HAD SPENT ANOTHER restless night, his dreams filled with visions of Oriel. In some she approved of what he was doing, in others she berated him—for installing another woman in her home, in her room, in her bed! A number of times he had awakened, thrashing against the sheets.

When day finally dawned, he awoke to the realization that he wanted it all to end. Strangely, considering how badly he had wanted it, he was growing tired of playing the avenging god. But if he didn't do it, who would? He couldn't just let them get away with what they had done. He *had* to continue. An eye for an eye, a tooth for a tooth . . . no matter what it took!

Stiffening his resolve, he dressed and presented himself at the door to Oriel's suite.

IT WAS TOO EARLY an hour for most of the guests to be up, but several had tumbled from their beds and made their way downstairs to the solarium. There in the traditional breakfast area of the house, they had gathered, one reading a newspaper, the other two conversing desultorily over coffee, toast and jam pots.

Paul and Allison's entrance brought an end to their peace.

Jean Anne was the first to notice them. Even at that hour her face was not free of heavy slashes of makeup and her jet black hair stood at attention with military precision.

She tapped Frank Alexander's wrist; he was sitting across from her. He, too, turned to face them, his knowing smile quickly surfacing.

"Well, well, well," he said. "Look who we have here. You always were an early riser, Paul. It seems as if your little friend is, too. Good morning, Magda."

The newspaper rustled and partially fell. From behind it Evan Sargent stared at them.

Allison's smile was tentative. "Good morning," she said.

The room was populated with a number of small, round glass-topped tables resting on wrought-iron pedestals. Chairs of matching wrought iron boasted pastel cushions of pale pink and mint green. A multitude of green plants, even more evident here than in the rest of the public rooms, brought the out-of-doors inside, just as did the sun shining through the lightly tinted glass walls.

A young girl in a beige dress appeared. "Coffee, miss? Or would you prefer tea? We also have fresh orange and apple juice."

"Apple juice," Allison decided.

"Coffee," Paul said.

The girl nodded and hurried over to a service table that was set against one wall. She was back in a moment with their requests.

Paul chose an empty table near the others. Allison, unwilling to be left standing, settled with him.

"Did you sleep well?" Frank asked. His words were directed to Allison.

She took a sip from her glass and smiled at the tangy sweetness. "Yes, I did, as a matter of fact. I feel much better this morning."

"Good. Possibly later we can take a walk down to the lake. It's a sight you shouldn't miss. There's nothing like it on your island, I'm quite sure."

"No," Allison murmured.

"I'm showing her the lake," Paul intervened.

Frank's amusement increased. "Another day, then? You wouldn't begrudge her a second look, would you Paul?"

Paul said nothing.

"Magda—" Jean Anne drew out the name as if testing it for proper usage.

Allison turned to look at her. In Jean Anne she didn't sense the degree of animosity she felt in the others. Jean Anne seemed an outsider, too.

"Tell me about your island," she said.

Allison's heart sank. She had learned what she could about Marabu, but she had always felt that this was one of her weaker points. Especially now, since Evan had actually been there. She couldn't afford to get even one tiny thing wrong.

"What do you want to know?" she hedged.

Jean Anne shrugged. "Oh—everything, I suppose. I'm curious."

"Well, it's beautiful... or at least, *I* think it's beautiful. The people are friendly. Very few tourists visit because it's not set up for them. And that's the way most of the people who live there want it to continue."

"How are the beaches?" Jean Anne questioned. She laughed lightly. "That's always important to someone from southern California."

Allison hesitated. "They're . . . nice."

"Isn't that a bit of an understatement?" Evan demanded, butting his way into the conversation. "Oriel thought they were the best kept secret in the Caribbean!"

Allison smiled tightly. "That's why I only said they were nice."

"She's got you there, Evan," Frank murmured.

Evan grumped and hid behind his newspaper again. But Allison knew that he continued to listen.

Jean Anne went on with her questioning. "And this convent . . . isn't an island an odd place to have one?"

"Our Lady of Mercy is almost two hundred years old. It was founded by a group of French sisters who were looking for seclusion in which to pray and do good works."

Paul had told her that the convent actually existed on the island. But it was a cloister and resisted any contact with the outside world. It could be breached, but he felt that it would take a fair amount of time.

"And you want to be one of them?" Jean Anne asked. To her, the idea must have seemed incredible.

"I have been one of them, unofficially."

"And you like it?"

Allison smiled. "I like it. But Sister Dominica encouraged me to make the most of this trip. She wants me to be certain before I begin taking my vows."

"This sounds like something from a book!" Frank exclaimed.

"You can say that again!" Evan rustled the newspaper, but stayed firmly behind it.

"A nun," Jean Anne breathed.

"Nuns are ordinary people," Allison defended. She didn't know any personally, but they had to be. It only stood to reason.

"But what about—" Jean Anne's words were quickly cut off.

"What about what?" Allison prompted.

"Well...men!"

Paul cleared his throat. "I think this has gone far enough, don't you? You're beginning to intrude."

Jean Anne threw Paul a defiant look. "When she came here, she had to expect that we'd be curious. What's the matter, Paul? Are you going to show her about sex, too, the same as you'll show her the lake?"

Paul immediately bridled. "That's enough, Jean Anne!"

"You couldn't get Oriel to look at you. Are you going to try it with her look-alike sister? And if you can carry it far enough, just think of all that lovely money you'll have to play with...not to mention having Dusty and me and all the others at your beck and call. Just like Oriel did!"

Paul scraped back his chair, bumping the table and spilling his coffee. "You foulmouthed little...!"

Allison reached out to stop him. "Paul, no... please."

"Paul, no... please," Jean Anne giggled, mimicking Allison.

Allison changed her estimation of the woman. She was just as acrimonious as the others. She was merely better at covering it.

When Jean Anne started to laugh Paul shook Allison's hand from his arm and stalked stiffly from the room, causing Jean Anne's laughter to grow even louder.

Frank's eyes rolled. "For heaven's sake, give it a rest. You put your blade in and twisted it, now leave it alone! I *am* trying to eat."

Jean Anne's laughter instantly dried up, and she turned a venomous glare on Frank before jumping up from the table to escape.

The room lapsed into an intense silence as soon as she had departed. Allison's hand remained curled around her glass of juice, but she didn't feel like drinking it any longer.

"You have to understand," Frank confided. "Jean Anne wasn't trying to get at you. It was Paul. She's had a thing for him ever since she first started coming here with Dusty, and she can't get him to look at her. Frustrates the hell out of her. She was jealous of Oriel, now she's got you to worry about. Poor thing."

Evan dropped all pretense of reading the paper. "Silly bitch," he declared with not an ounce of compassion.

Suddenly Allison had to get outside, to breathe some fresh air. Pushing away from the table, she said, "I think I'll— Excuse me, I want to—"

"Are you all right?" Frank asked, immediately concerned.

"I'm fine. Really. I just..."

"Oh, all right... *go!*" Frank sat back, switching instantly to irritability. "Don't let me stop you. You don't know me from Adam, do you? Just as I don't know you. Go ahead, run after him. Cool his fevered brow. Offer yourself up on the altar of his virility. Gad! I can't understand what women see in him! Evan, hand over the keys to your liquor cabinet. Yes, I know your rule," he snapped. "But I feel the need for liquid refreshment now, not noon!"

Allison hurried from the room. So many emotions, pulling in so many different directions. If she wasn't careful, she could be torn apart.

ALLISON FOUND HER WAY to the front terrace and then to the path that she and Paul had used the evening before. As soon as the house was swallowed by the trees, she felt an indescribable relief and was able to slow her retreat. For such a beautiful structure, architecturally, the passions within it were like a festering poison. Anger, envy, hatred, greed... those negative emotions battered all who entered.

She leaned back against a tall pine and tried to collect her breath, her thoughts. For a moment she had truly been frightened. She wasn't accustomed to displays of such raw emotion.

Jealousy and greed played no part in the world her grandfather had carved for them, and anger was merely a fleeting thunderclap. He had worked for the same janitorial supply company for forty-two years, raised one son and one granddaughter. Money had been important, but only to provide the necessities of life. It was never something to hoard. Or to fight about.

Possibly that was why she and her grandfather were in this situation now. But if faced with the troubles in her life or the troubles in Oriel's friends', she would choose her life any time. So, she knew, would her grandfather.

She pushed away from the tree's slender trunk and continued down the trail, past the point where she and Paul had turned back yesterday. She needed the exercise, and she needed to be on her own—to settle her nerves, to settle her mind.

She bent to pick up a pine cone and examined it. It was so simple and yet so complicated in its structure. Just as life could sometimes be. She could imagine how difficult it had been for Oriel and Paul to grow up amid such conflict. No wonder Paul resented the others so deeply. His dislike must have carried back a number of years.

Neither was she surprised by Jean Anne's attraction to Paul. Or by her spitefulness. It wasn't unusual that love and hate could quite easily coexist.

Allison tossed the pine cone away and continued her walk, the fresh, pungent odor of the forest her companion.

Unexpectedly around a curve in the trail she came upon Paul. He was standing at the edge of a clearing...a meadow, actually, that sloped downhill to another line of trees then on to the lake.

At once she halted. From the bleakness of his expression and the dispirited slump to his shoulders, she knew that he remained oblivious to her presence. She watched him for a moment, surprised. His facade had dropped, showing that he was very much human, not machine. Spiteful words and acts actually hurt him. Then she started to back away, knowing that he wouldn't appreciate her intrusion. But a twig broke underfoot.

At once he swung around, spotted her and challenged, "What are you doing here? Were you following me?"

Allison shook her head. "No. I—I just came for a walk."

His dark eyes bored into her, trying to gauge if she was telling the truth, what she had seen. She withstood his intent inspection.

He relaxed slightly, but still retained the frown he normally wore when around her. "Did anything unusual happen after I left?"

"It depends upon what you mean by 'unusual.' But no, I suppose not."

Paul turned back to the meadow, silently studying the thin grasses as they swayed in the light breeze.

Allison glanced back along the path she had taken. She could leave now, she supposed. Ignoring her was always his signal that she was dismissed. Or she could stay there. Her choices were simple.

Then words seemed to burst from him, surprising her by both their tone and their content. "You can see how miserable they made her life! It's no wonder that she— I tried to help, but—"

She felt helpless in the face of his sudden confidence and also by his anguish. She said, "I'm sure you did all you could."

"You believe that?" He turned to face her again, his dark eyes tortured—seeking her, finding her, making her feel...

Allison became rooted to the spot. She didn't understand what was happening, but something had changed; something had shifted. "Yes," she managed.

He was silent for another long moment, a moment that seemed to last an eternity. Then he murmured huskily, "You're so much like her. The color of your hair, your skin, your eyes..."

He didn't seem to see her anymore. He was seeing someone else, someone locked inside his own vision.

Still, an all-enveloping warmth radiated throughout Allison's body and she took an instinctive step back.

"No," he whispered, "don't go. Not now. Not when—" A spasm passed over his face.

Allison's body began to tingle. She couldn't have moved if she tried. Everything seemed so unreal. Like in a dream. And yet not. Her breathing had quickened, but she couldn't get enough air. Her teeth wanted to chatter, but she wasn't cold.

Golden sunbeams reflected upon the waving grasses of the meadow. The two of them, at its edge, remained in shadow. A bird on a limb nearby called to its mate.

"Oriel?" Paul breathed, taking a hesitant step toward her.

Allison watched him as faithfully as a doe must watch a hunter, unable to help herself even though knowing that certain annihilation would follow.

When he had closed the space between them, he reached out to very gently touch the soft, smooth skin of her cheek.

Allison's eyelids fluttered.

Paul watched intently as he threaded his fingers into her hair, spreading them through the red-gold silkiness. His other hand then moved to the base of her neck, where her pulse, beating like a wild thing's, throbbed beneath his thumb.

"Oh, God," he whispered. Then finally his gentleness ended. Tipping her head back, he lowered his mouth so that it could plunder hers, drinking thirstily of the nectar which he had too long been denied, calling silently to her, urging her to respond.

The sane part of Allison's mind screamed at her to break away. That this was not supposed to be happening. But the rest of her was so caught up in the moment that she didn't care anymore. The hot intensity of his kisses, of his body pressed tightly against hers, the insistency of his hands drawing her even closer, were almost more than she could bear. He had held himself aloof for so long, distanced himself so completely—*fascinated* her so completely. It didn't matter why this was happening, or why she was welcoming it. She just was!

Paul urged her to a softened bed of pine needles a short distance off the trail, the heat of his body transferring his desire, the strength of his arms guiding her down. Allison spread her fingers over his shoulders, sensitive to the muscles working beneath his jacket, which he soon discarded. Then he quickly abandoned his shirt so that she could touch him even more intimately. He bent over her, concentrating on the buttons that secured her bodice. "I love you, Oriel," he murmured brokenly. "I love you—"

This time the name registered deeply on Allison's consciousness and she automatically stiffened.

Paul didn't seem to notice. He continued to work on the tiny buttons, finally succeeding in freeing them. Then he tugged the loosened material from her shoulders and stroked the graceful curve of her breast.

Allison didn't know how she could have let things go this far! Humiliation raced into her cheeks as she fought to cover herself. "No, Paul. No," she rasped tightly. "Don't. Please!"

Her continued resistance finally reached him. He pulled back, blinking. And for a moment he just stared at her. Then, his chest heaving, a racking shudder passed over his muscular frame and he uttered a groan of such intense despair that it forever lacerated the serenity of Allison's soul.

Forgetting everything that had passed before, Allison instantly reached out to him, responding to his terrible pain. But either he didn't see her offering or he didn't want it. On stumbling feet, he gathered his shirt and tie and jacket and crashed his way across the meadow.

A choking sob tore its way from Allison's throat as she watched him go, a tiny echo to his own.

Then with shaken limbs and shaken heart she rearranged her clothing and hurried in the direction of the house.

Chapter Eight

Purely for self-protection, Allison acted as if nothing had happened. After encountering no one as she made her way to her room, she changed her dirt-smudged dress for another, firmed her constitution and went downstairs again.

Of Paul, she saw nothing—a fact which caused intensely mixed feelings. In the cool light of reason, what had happened between them did seem more a dream than reality. And yet she knew that it was fact. She had thought all along that Paul loved Oriel, sensed it without the words ever needing to be said. Randall had even confirmed it, in his own cautious way. So why should she be so surprised that since she looked so much like Oriel he would act accordingly. Except she also sensed that Paul had never acted upon the love he felt for Oriel, at least not physically, and her suspicion had been borne up by Jean Anne. So why act on it now? With her? And, more important, why had she let him?

The house party had separated into different groups. Some of the guests were taking dips in the heated pool, others were playing tennis. Still others were sunning themselves on the rear terrace, lying in chaise lounges, *collecting rays,* as Dusty explained while inviting her to join them. With his red hair and pale coloring, what skin he had exposed was slathered in suntan lotion. Dusty's sunning companion was Mary LeBlanc.

"Won't the nuns allow you to wear anything but a dress?" Mary complained, looking disdainfully at Allison's choice of clothing. She, herself, was wearing a tennis outfit, probably waiting for her turn to play.

"I didn't bring holiday clothes," Allison said. "I didn't realize I'd be needing them."

Mary's top lip curled. "Is that a slam at us, dear? Because if it is, it's a mistake. Oriel had this little get-together every year. She wouldn't want us to do without it now, just because she's no longer able to...well, attend. She loved these parties. Loved to watch her little line of marionettes. Pull a string here, pull a string there...watch us dance. She's probably in heaven right now, watching us and laughing."

"What makes you think she's in heaven?" Dusty quipped.

"You're right!" Mary chortled with approval. "There's a much better place. But I didn't want to sully Magda's little ears."

"You didn't like Oriel?" Allison probed.

Mary's laughter stopped. "I didn't say that."

"Then I don't understand. What you just said . . ."

"You'd understand if you'd really known her," Mary dismissed, then motioned to a nearby table. "Dusty, be a dear and hand me the lotion. I think my nose is getting burned."

Dusty did as he was asked, then struggled to his feet. "I think I'd better find some cover. I've had enough. It's the altitude, I think. My skin can't take the sun here."

Mary squirted a drop of lotion onto her fingertips. "Darling, you could get sunburned in a sea fog."

"At least that was *something* Oriel and I had in common," Dusty claimed proudly.

"Mother Nature took care of that problem for me," Mary said. Then, at Dusty's blank look, she explained, "Our sex? We're both female?"

"Oh," Dusty said, blinking.

Mary shook her head as he walked away. "Men can be dense, but Dusty excels. He's going to pay for his few minutes in the sun. He's already burned."

Allison could already feel the sun warming her own exposed skin. "I should go inside as well," she said. It was also a good excuse to not continue the conversation.

"Yes," Mary said, her eyes narrowing. "You do have Oriel's skin, Oriel's eyes...it's like looking at her in the flesh again. From ten years ago."

"I've seen a photograph."

"Then you can understand how startled we all were when Paul introduced you."

"Is that all it was...startled?"

An obstinate look settled on Mary's unremarkable face. "Should it have been anything else? I don't think so. We jumped when she said jump, danced when she said dance. I have nothing to feel guilty about."

"I never said you did," Allison said softly.

"Paul does. He blames us for everything! We're going to check, you know. We're not just going to take his word, or his documents. It's too important. We've all waited far too long to..."

Frank ambled onto the terrace from the house, a partially filled glass held loosely in his hand. "For *what* have you waited too long, Mary Dearest? For someone to tell you how lovely you are? How sweet? How precious? How the songbirds wait each morning for you to appear before they give voice to their melodious tributes?"

Mary's displeasure increased. "You're drunk, Frank!"

"No, I'm not. I'm happy! There's a difference. You should try it sometime." He saluted Allison with his glass. "It's an absolutely wonderful morning, I'm surrounded by beautiful women. I have everything in life I could possibly want!"

"Except a hit play," Mary reminded nastily.

Frank clasped his free hand to his chest. "You wound me, Mary. I try to forget, but I can always count upon you to remember. To you, my good woman, I give eternal thanks!''

"Oh, go away!" she said crossly. "I don't feel like putting up with you this morning."

"You never feel like putting up with me."

"Neither does anyone else! Take the hint!"

A shadow of hurt passed over Frank's face, but he was quick to cover it. "I'll take the hint when the rest of you do. As long as you're here, I'm here. Remember that."

"Go away, Frank!" Mary turned onto her side, deliberately facing away from him.

Frank stared at her for several long seconds before remembering Allison's presence. He glanced at her, downed the remainder of his drink, and said, "I need a refill. Want to come with me, Magda? The temperature's dropped about fifty degrees out here. You might get frostbite."

Allison followed him inside. He led the way to the library. The room, though large, was surprisingly comfortable.

Frank went straight to a line of bottles secured behind beveled glass doors. He paused before pouring himself another drink.

"Want something?" he asked.

Allison shook her head.

"Are you shocked that I do?" he asked.

"No."

"But you'd rather that I didn't. My wife was exactly the same. She thought she could change me. She knew of my fondness, you see, before we got married. But, alas, I can't be changed. In the end, she gave up and divorced me. Found someone else she could make over. He's written a screenplay, I believe, which is actually being produced. Annette will be pleased.'' He took a sip and made a face. ''Actually, I hate the taste of this stuff.''

''Then why do you drink it?''

''Because it makes me feel good. Why else? Why does anyone do anything?''

''Mary mentioned something about a play. Your play?'' As Magda, Allison was supposed to act as if she didn't know anything about these people, only what Oriel had written. Which would, in turn, make them wonder just how much she truly did know. Paul's goal was to keep them guessing.

''I write plays,'' Frank confirmed.

''Anything familiar?''

''You mean like on Broadway?'' He laughed. ''No. But, don't forget, you're supposed to have been raised in a convent. How's a little convent girl going to know about Broadway?''

Allison smiled. ''I didn't enter the convent until I was fifteen. But we do have newspapers, and radio and a little television. We keep up with the world.''

''Why?''

''In order to pray for it.''

Frank's mustache twitched. ''I need a lot of prayer.''

"I'll remember that . . . if I go back. And even if I don't!"

Frank was still smiling as he collapsed into a chair. "Sit down. I promise I won't bite. And I'll tell you a little story. It's about a man who's squandered most of his talent. Sometimes he regrets it—other times he doesn't. But he has a play, you see. A play that he thinks is better than anything that's out there. It was written when he was a young man—barely dry behind the ears—at a time when passions ran high, as well as ambition. He couldn't get it backed, though. No one believed in the play but him. Oh, he had a few nibbles, but nothing serious. He had a few minor successes with other plays, but it wasn't enough to make him forget his first love. Then he met a man—a rich, powerful man, who read the play, saw something in it and promised to see it through all the terrors to opening night." Frank grew silent, staring down into his glass.

"But it didn't work out that way. The man kept promising and promising, stringing the playwright along. It would almost happen, then the man would pull back. Over and over. It came so close! The playwright finally had enough and offered the play to someone else, but the rich man was so powerful that no one else would take it. He spread rumors about the playwright's drinking, about his unreliability. So ultimately the playwright came back to the rich man, hat in hand, shall we say, and begged him to reconsider.

The man said he would, but he left the playwright hanging."

"My father... and you," Allison said softly.

Frank shrugged. "Damien promised to make provisions for my play in his will, if I'd jump every time he said jump. I agreed. But when it passed to Oriel, she wanted me to jump some more."

"Why?" Allison asked, frowning.

Frank shrugged again. "To be perverse? Our Oriel was a bit more complicated than some people think."

Paul, Allison acknowledged, but she didn't say his name.

"Didn't she like you?" she asked.

"I would say she did. We had an affair once, a long time ago."

Allison was surprised. Did Paul know?

"Could it be that, then?" she asked. "Could that be the reason she refused?"

Frank swirled what remained of his drink. "We were friends, as much as anyone could be friends with her. Didn't she tell you about me?"

"I knew you wrote plays," Allison confessed.

"And probably a lot more. Why did you let me drone on?"

Allison smiled. "It's always best to let people say things in their own way."

Frank looked at her carefully, his eyes having finally taken on the cloudy haze of inebriation. "You're a lot smarter than I've given you credit for," he said slowly.

Allison's attention was caught by the sound of people coming down the hall. Several voices could be heard raised in argument. One of them belonged to Paul. Allison's stomach tightened. She would rather put off seeing him again until later. Much later. How could she face him when both of them would remember—

She might not have spent energy worrying. When Paul saw that she was already in the room, his dark eyes flicked over her without emotion. As far as he was concerned, it seemed, what had happened on the trail was forgotten.

Allison's cheeks grew warm as twin sensations battled within her: shame, because she had given those moments importance and he had not, and anger, that he could be so callous.

Or was it all an act? Allison examined him more closely. Beneath his calm demeanor, she could sense strain. His body was tensed, his expression disciplined rather than detached. He glanced at her again and memory flooded over her because, for a split second, his dark eyes had blazed. It was enough to make her knees go weak. Somehow she was able to control her reaction by quickly looking away, by counting from one to one hundred, by firmly telling herself that she had to hold on! Then she noticed that the others were talking, and that Frank was woozily trying to defend himself.

Without really thinking, she jumped to his aid. "Leave him alone!" she directed Jennifer Clark. "He's not bothering you."

"He *bothers* me every time I have to look at him," Jennifer replied. "Jim, do something!"

Jim quickly did as his wife ordered. He tried, unsuccessfully, to catch Frank's arm. "Why don't you take a little nap," he suggested. "Then after dinner you'll feel better."

"He'll only feel better when he's six feet under!" Jennifer said coldly.

"Like Oriel?" Paul challenged.

To her credit, Jennifer looked slightly startled, then bluffing, she said, "Stop pouncing on everything I say, Paul. You know I didn't mean it that way."

"Then stop picking on Frank."

Frank continued to evade Jim's attempts to contain him. "*You,* Paul? Defending *me?* Is the world coming to an end?"

"Stay out of this," Jennifer snapped at Frank.

"I won't! I . . ."

Allison stood up. "Frank, please, go with Jim. Just this once? Possibly you will feel better after a rest."

She was the object of shocked stares from both the Clarks.

Frank gave her a blurry salute. "An angel . . . or a wraith. I'm not sure which."

"An *angel!*" Jennifer snorted. "Of all the ridiculous . . . !"

Paul interrupted, "You've won for the moment. Why don't you keep quiet?"

Jennifer glared at him.

Finally Jim succeeded in taking hold of Frank's arm, and pulling him along, he crossed over to his wife. "You wanted to change out of those tennis things before lunch, didn't you, dear? Why don't you come with us now? Lunch will be served shortly."

Jennifer let herself be led away. "I still say it's ridiculous! This entire *affair* is ridiculous! For her to think that she can just sashay in here and take everything that we've worked so hard for— And *you* call her an angel?" She again turned her virulence upon Frank.

Paul walked to the door and without a word closed the others outside. For the first few seconds, Jennifer's voice could still be heard as she harangued Frank and her husband. Then slowly it lessened and the huge room fell into silence.

"I've warned you about him," Paul said slowly, breaking the quiet.

Allison was greatly aware of their isolation. She had been alone with him numerous times before, even lived in the same apartment, but the situation had changed.

"I was only doing what you asked," she said.

"He called you an angel."

"He also wondered if I was a ghost! Isn't that what you want? To keep them confused? He was telling me about his play. About the way Damien kept stalling him."

"He complained about Oriel, too, didn't he?"

"Did you know that he and Oriel were once lovers?"

Allison hadn't meant for that to come out quite so baldly! But the words just slipped out.

Paul stiffened. "He told you that?"

Allison nodded.

"You did have quite a little talk, didn't you? Yes, I knew. I knew about it when it was happening. Oriel was on the rebound from her second divorce and Frank kept coming around, offering her a shoulder to cry on."

"You couldn't stop her?"

Paul's look was resentful. "I couldn't stop her from doing anything. She wouldn't listen to me."

Allison recognized the hurt behind his words. "What did you do then?" she asked softly. It must have been a terrible time for him.

"Nothing. I wanted to kill Frank . . . but I didn't." Paul's gaze turned inward. He remembered talking to Oriel then, trying to get her to see reason. But even at that fairly early stage, she no longer seemed to trust him. He had tried to tell her that *he* would never hurt her, but she was too upset to listen. Too involved with Frank. Frank! He forced himself to continue, "That's why I've warned you to watch out for him. I don't want the same thing to happen to you."

Allison frowned. "It takes two to have an affair. All the blame can't be placed on him."

"Oriel was vulnerable! He took advantage of her."

"Possibly he was vulnerable, too."

"Frank's never been vulnerable a day in his life!"

"I don't believe that."

"Neither did Oriel!"

Allison had a comeback ready to deliver, but she thought better of using it. Paul had a blind spot where Oriel was concerned. Nothing she said would ever convince him. *She didn't know Oriel*—he would say. And he would be right. But had he? Really?

Allison looked away. She had to remember that she was here to do a job, not to try to fix things—either for Paul or for anyone else. She had enough trouble on her plate without adding more. All she had to do was get through the next series of days....

Paul reached out to bring her chin around, but stilled his hand before it made contact.

Sensing what had almost happened, Allison lifted her gaze and in seconds the atmosphere in the room grew taut.

Paul tried desperately to control his emotions. What had happened earlier on the pathway had been a mistake, a terrible mistake. He couldn't let it happen again! And yet... it was almost more than he could bear! He was drowning in the haunting greenness of her eyes, in his remembrance of the softness of her lips, of her body. All he could think about was that he had been given another chance. A chance to make things right, to tell her of his love... to make her believe him!

Almost of its own volition his hand started to move again. He wanted to touch her more than he wanted life! Then suddenly she twisted away, turned her back on him.

In mounting confusion his hand dropped. His heart was knocking in his chest, his body was burning with desire. But he forced himself to realize that *she* wasn't Oriel. That she was the woman he had hired to play the *part* of Oriel. No... Magda! He had only wanted her to look like Oriel so that she would be convincing. Like a god, he had created her... by poking and prodding and pushing this way and that, until he was satisfied with his handiwork. But had he done his job too well?

Paul tried to put the thought from his mind, but stubbornly it wouldn't budge. He looked at the woman again. Even from behind she reminded him of Oriel. He tried desperately to contain his emotions. Finally he cleared his throat. "Lunch will be served in approximately thirty minutes. I believe we should be present. Do you have an objection?"

She shook her head. Still she didn't turn to look at him.

Sudden anger sparked deep within Paul's heart to blend with his other churning emotions. He didn't know if he was angry with her or with himself or with this crazy situation. Possibly after all of this was over, he would find himself a good psychologist and try to figure everything out. That is, if he wasn't already bouncing off the walls of some padded cell!

LUNCH, IN ALLISON'S opinion, should have merited combat pay. Linguistic scuffles abounded, between which periodic verbal missiles were launched from one side of the table to the other.

If these people had developed strong friendships after all their years of knowing one another, it was difficult to tell. They seemed prepared to argue about everything! Who had said what to whom, in regard to which, upon which day...they were like children, jostling for a better place in line.

"I still say that I'm the one who told Oriel to purchase all those shares of stock when the market was down," one claimed.

"No, you didn't. I did! I called her on Sunday night. You waited until Monday afternoon, and by that time the stock had already risen five points," another countered.

"And who told you?"

"It certainly wasn't you!"

It was a relief to have the meal end.

Allison had done her best to remain invisible, and to his credit, Paul had deflected most of the hostility aimed toward her. But Paul was another sore point.

If she thought that he had been distant with her before their arrival, it was nothing to the distance he now seemed intent upon keeping between them. At least that was the way he had acted from the time he called at her door a few minutes before noon to accompany her downstairs, as well as throughout the meal itself...even if he did stir himself periodically to inter-

vene on her behalf. To do that, though, was to protect
his interests. She was his trump card, his ace in the
hole.

The group again split up after lunch. Where Paul
went, Allison had no idea. One moment he was
standing nearby, the next he was gone. She found
herself sitting in the library with Dusty Martin and
Jean Anne, who soon told Dusty that she was going to
their room for a nap and that she didn't want to be
disturbed. On her way out she gave Allison a superior
look, which she thought Dusty didn't see. But when
Allison turned toward him, he was smiling.

"She doesn't like you very much, I'm afraid," he
said.

"Does anyone?" Allison asked.

"*Should* anyone?" Dusty shot back. Then, groan-
ing, he leaned his head back against the chair cushion
and closed his eyes. "Never mind, don't answer. I'm
tired of fighting. The entire meal was ruined because
of it. Why is it always the same in this house, with
these people?"

Allison gazed at the familiar face, at the little-boy
features under the thatch of orange-red hair. They
looked weathered with years now, but they still remained basically the same.

"Was that a rhetorical question?" she asked.

"Yes."

"Because if it wasn't, I might have an answer."

Dusty pried open one eye. "Fire away. I saw you at
the meal. You were watching everyone. What are your

conclusions?'' The other eye opened and he sat up. "It's not as if what you think doesn't hold weight. *If* what you say is true, one day you're going to hold all our lives in those pretty little hands of yours. You'll be able to do with us as you please. Just like Oriel. A very heady experience.''

"I don't understand how everyone let themselves get into such a position in the first place!" Allison complained, earnestly wondering.

"Talent!" he replied. Then he smiled slowly, explaining, "I mean it! Damien loved to surround himself with talented people because he was so unimaginative himself. He collected artists of one sort or another the way other people collect stamps. Some got away, others didn't. We're the ones who didn't.''

"You could now," Allison said.

"It's become a habit."

"But if it's ruining your lives—"

"You think we should just pick up and leave? Stand on our own two feet and march away. Poor, no doubt, but proud? Well, it doesn't work that way in real life, sweetheart. When you're poor, you don't eat very well. I've tried it. I didn't grow up with nice clothes and the wherewithal to hold on to a woman like Jean Anne. I worked hard for the little successes that I've had. But it all fell apart after a couple of years. Then Damien came along... Do you know what the rights to a song are? Well, Damien bought my rights from me when I was down and out. *He* controlled the songs I wrote. That *I* wrote! If someone wanted to make a recording of my work, they had to go to him for permission. They paid *him*." Dusty's lips thinned in bitterness at the memory. "When Damien died, the rights passed to Oriel. At first I thought she'd be better...that she'd let me have them back, just like it said she could in Damien's will. She agreed, then she backed out. And she wouldn't change her mind, not even when I told her how her father had cheated me. She..."

"He paid you for them, didn't he?" Allison interrupted.

"Yes—but not enough! Not for what they came to be worth! How was I supposed to know that my work would get popular again? I'm not a fortune-teller!"

"Neither was my father."

"But he was a cheat!" Dusty said heatedly. "And I wasn't the only one he cheated. Talk to Roger. Ask him about *Spencer's Way!* Ask him how Damien wormed his way into owning the film and then how he refused to let it go when at least three different video companies wanted to release it to the home market. And how Oriel wouldn't consider doing it, either. *Spencer's Way* is a classic! It could make a fortune for Roger and Mary! Revive his career!

"And Jim!" he continued. "Damien contracted with Jim to help him write his autobiography. It ended up that Damien didn't write a word of it. Jim did all the work. And the book hit it big! A company was hot to film it...there were negotiations. Jim even managed to get hold of a percentage. But would Damien allow it to be made? No! Neither would Oriel. She said she was afraid it would reflect badly on her father. But that wasn't it. She just wanted to be nasty to Jim. The interest is still there to film it, but—''

"Why did you stay?" Allison asked. "Why did any of you stay, if you disliked them so much?"

Dusty shook his head. "I don't know...you want the truth? It's this life-style. It gets in your blood."

"Is that why you accepted Oriel's check each month?"

Dusty looked stunned. "How do you know about that?"

Allison had decided to go to another level with Dusty. With each of them, she would pretend to a different understanding of the situation. "I've already explained. Oriel and I exchanged letters. She told me."

"She told you a hell of a lot!"

"Just what she thought I should know."

"Why? Was she planning to share?" He gave a short bark of laughter. "Oriel...sharing! What a joke! The money she gave me was a pittance—a mere pittance!"

"What if she was?" Allison asked.

His laughter stopped. "You mean she really was planning to share?"

Allison shook her head sadly. "I remember you, Mr. Martin. I remember your songs and your television show. They were even popular on Marabu. I was a little girl then, but I remember."

"Not that little, surely?" She had pricked his pride.

Allison smiled slightly. "Well, possibly not." She hummed the beginning notes of a melody before softly starting to sing the words.

Dusty grinned and took up the next verse.

They finished the song together, by which time, both were laughing.

"You *do* remember!" Dusty cried. "That was always my favorite, too. Do you know, I wrote that in fifteen minutes riding in a subway! It came to me all in a rush!"

"Why don't you try to do it again?"

Dusty's head fell back against the cushions, his face looking much older than it had when he was singing. "That part of my life is over. I write jingles now. For singing toilets and happy drains."

"Have you tried?" she asked.

"Of course I've tried! What do you think?"

"That maybe you should try again. You never know what might happen."

Dusty sighed. "You've got a Mary Poppins syndrome. Comes from living in a convent too long. You have to realize how the big bad world works. Otherwise it's going to eat you up."

"I'm not worried," Allison claimed softly.

Dusty's gaze moved over her. "Maybe you should be," he said, getting to his feet, "if you're planning to hang around here for long."

Allison remained still after Dusty had left the room, absorbing the import of his words.

All too soon, though, she became aware of something watching her. Obeying instinct, she looked up... to meet the feral glass eyes of the ram.

Was it her imagination? Or did the animal look as if it was about to leap off the wall and attack?

Chapter Nine

Allison did her best to avoid Frank when he came downstairs later that afternoon. In fact, she did her best to avoid all of them. After that chilling experience in the library—was it a threat that Dusty had issued?—she decided to take Paul's advice and delay her next appearance.

To aid in that decision, she made a much more detailed exploration of the public areas of the house. When they weren't outside or in their own rooms, the house guests seemed to gravitate to certain areas—the dining room, the solarium or the library. She was sure of privacy as she wandered in these lesser-used rooms.

Just as everywhere else, they were magnificent, boasting only the very best of style and decor. She even made her way into the kitchen, a roomy area filled with wide work spaces and all the newest gadgets. She spoke with Mrs. Wainwright, the housekeeper, and two of her helpers, who were friendly, but the rumor of her identity must have spread because it was easy to see that she made them nervous. Were they afraid that she was making a surprise inspection? Checking on their habits and their abilities, with thought to a future decision as to whether they would be kept on or not? Allison was able to sympathize with their jitteriness, and she quickly left the room to let them have some peace.

It was after her retreat from the kitchen that she came upon a room she had missed earlier. Much smaller and tucked away from the others, it had a different feel. Books lined one wall, but they were not there just for show. These books had been read and reread until the spines on some were worn and battered. Two overlarge chairs of rich brown leather were drawn up on either side of a freestanding lamp. A massive desk, complementary to the walnut paneling, displayed a variety of pipes on a stand. It was a man's study. Damien's? Allison couldn't picture Evan in this room.

She walked to the desk and shyly fingered a pen set. "He was quite a gentleman," Frank said, coming into the room.

Surprised by his appearance, Allison jumped, highly aware that she was trespassing.

"I thought you didn't like him," she said, trying to recover.

"I didn't. But he was still intriguing. So is anyone with that much power. Have you ever seen a picture of him?"

Allison shook her head.

Frank smiled as he came to take her hand and lead her to a wall where a wide range of memorabilia was displayed. At first it was difficult for Allison to focus on what he wished her to see, there were so many photographs and plaques. But Frank solved the problem by switching on a light that topped a medium-sized portrait. Allison drew a quick breath.

The painting was of a man somewhere in his early fifties, his dark red hair not yet having lightened, his frame still moderately slender. Sharp intelligent eyes were set above a strong chin and a mouth that brooked no nonsense. He had the look of a person accustomed to making hard judgments. But it was the young woman at his side who truly startled Allison: Oriel! Younger than she had ever seen her, without the hardened edge. It was like looking at a painting of herself! Paul had given them exactly the same style of hair, makeup and dress. She groped for something to steady her.

"Are you all right?" Frank asked, instantly solicitous. "I didn't mean to upset you. I never thought that seeing him would have such an impact." Frank assisted her into one of the leather chairs, then looked around for another aid. "Would you like a drink?" he asked, and not waiting for a reply, started for the row of half-filled decanters hidden on a narrow shelf of the bookcase.

Allison shook her head. "No. No, thank you."

"Well, I would," Frank said. "I'll even double up on your behalf."

"Frank," Allison called, stopping him. "Not for me. Please. Don't do it for me."

Frank looked at her, then looked at the decanters, his tongue darting out to wipe his lips, as if he could already taste the liquor. His gaze slid reluctantly away. "Water, then. I'll get you water."

"I'm fine. Really. It was just . . . a shock."

Frank came back to rest on one knee at her side. He took hold of her cold hands. "You were so pale. I thought you were going to pass out!"

"I'm stronger than I look," Allison murmured.

"But I'd feel terrible if I thought that anything I had done had . . ."

"Frank!" Paul's voice rang out like a shot.

Both Frank and Allison flinched, turning startled eyes to see him standing in the doorway. He returned their looks with angry menace.

Frank's hand tightened on hers before he released it and slowly rose to his feet.

Allison struggled to stand as well, aware that she was the cause of most of Paul's anger. He kept warning her to stay away from this man and he kept finding them together.

"There's no need to shout," Frank said soothingly, having regained some of his aplomb.

"What are you doing here?" Paul demanded. There was no lessening of his menace.

"Magda felt faint—"

"Why? What did you do to her?"

A flash of irritation passed over Frank's features. "I didn't *do* anything," he denied.

"Then why were you apologizing?"

"That wasn't meant for you to hear."

"Too bad. I heard."

"And immediately jumped to the wrong conclusion."

"Paul!" Allison cried. "He didn't do anything!"

"Stop defending him!" Paul directed.

"I'm not defending him. I'm telling the truth!"

"Exactly what do you know about the truth?"

"See here!" Frank stepped forward. "Don't take your anger out on her when I'm the person you have a grievance with."

"I've had a grievance with you for a long time, Frank," Paul said coldly.

"Ever since you were a boy... I know!"

"And do you know why I've been angry?"

"I don't dare guess."

Allison didn't think that now was a good time to mock, and she was right. Paul took several long strides, reached for Frank's lapels and jerked him forward, almost off his feet. Frank's mockery fast disappeared.

"You don't have to guess, Frank," Paul said huskily. "I'll tell you—it's because not content to wallow alone in your sickness, you had to spread it to Oriel. You were always handy with a bottle, weren't you? Pouring a drink for her, encouraging her to take another, then another... Did you introduce her to the pills, too? Did you think it was fun to have someone else share in your degradation? Well, I didn't think it was *fun*, Frank. I had to watch while you and the others egged her on. I had to watch as little by little she slid into the gutter alongside you. Do you think that was easy, Frank? *Do you?*" Paul gave him a rattling shake.

Frank brought up his forearms and in a surprise move, knocked Paul's hands away. "You don't know what you're talking about, Paul. You never have."

"I *saw* you, Frank!"

"Sometimes what you think you see and what's really going on are two different things! Grow up, Paul. Open your eyes!"

"I *am* grown up! My eyes *are* open! That's why I'm not going to let it happen again! Stay away from her, Frank. Don't look at her, don't talk to her, don't go anywhere near her!"

Frank glanced at Allison, who had grown even paler. "Doesn't the lady have anything to say about this?"

"No!" Paul ruled.

Allison started to protest, but caught sight of Frank's slight shake of his head. He was giving her a well-considered warning. She remained silent.

Whether or not Paul caught the exchange, Allison didn't know. She looked at him with wounded eyes. Sometimes he made her so angry! And yet she was coming to feel such compassion for him. What he had gone through had been tragic—to watch the person he loved destroy herself!

Frank spoke quietly. "I've learned one thing in life, Paul. Even if I haven't followed it—it's not healthy to live in the past, to cling to old loves and old hurts. In order to move forward, a person has to let go. Hate only twists you up inside. Sometimes love does, too."

"Go to hell," Paul snarled bitterly.

Frank shrugged and walked away.

Allison looked after him. Then her gaze switched mutely to Paul.

He returned her look for several brittle seconds before he, too, turned on his heels and left. His exit was as abrupt as his entrance.

SOMEHOW ALLISON SURVIVED dinner that evening. Paul made no appearance, so she was left on her own to deal with the others. And Frank was of little help, having imbibed much too freely during the afternoon. As quickly as she could, she escaped to her room.

A gilded cage... Was that an apt description of this room? Had it become that for Oriel as well? Had Oriel, too, wanted to escape—to fly away and never come back?

Allison knew she had only a limited time here. For Oriel, life must have stretched like some long, dark tunnel.

But Oriel had been in control, hadn't she? She had been the one who made all the others jump? She could have changed things if she wanted. But what if Frank and Dusty and Mary had told her the truth? What if Oriel was more than just a little like her father, enjoying having the others tied to her, enjoying pulling them this way and that, testing just how far she could go. That was the exact opposite of Paul's impression. Who could be believed? Who was the real Oriel? And why should it make any difference to her... Allison?

Allison slowly turned, taking in every aspect of the room. She had sensed something of Oriel's personality here before. Would it be possible for her to discover more?

Forcing herself to walk to the bed, she slipped off her shoes, climbed onto the soft covers and lay down. Her head rested on the pillows that Oriel had used, her eyes saw what Oriel had seen. On the ceiling a delicate grouping of angels cavorted in celestial play, while around the bed the four wooden posts stood silent guard.

Allison closed her eyes, trying to imagine what it would be like to own this house, to have been Damien Woodrich's daughter, to be Evan Sargent's wife... to own two other houses in this state alone, and to command so many other lives.

She couldn't imagine it. It was too far removed from the reality of her days. Allison sat up.

To one side of the bed was a nightstand. On it was a porcelain lamp, several small framed photos—again of people she didn't recognize—and a book. The book had been on the bestseller list several months before.

It was marked by a business card about halfway through.

Allison flipped the book open, exposing the card. It bore the embossed name of a drug-rehabilitation center, in all likelihood the institute where Oriel had died. Scrawled upon it, was a name.

A wave of sadness washed over Allison. Time had stood still only between the pages of this book.

Driven by curiosity, she opened the nightstand's only drawer and began to search through the contents. The top layer was the usual bits and pieces of everyone's private life: tissues and notions and various over-the-counter medications. But it was beneath this layer, concealed by a folded scarf, that Allison found a matching set of slender suede-covered volumes. Five were bound by a thin red ribbon; the sixth was free.

Her movements were cautious as she extracted her prize. Without even opening them, she sensed that she had stumbled onto something of tremendous importance—something that would give her insight into Oriel. From the way they were hidden, not left to casual view, they must have meant a great deal to her.

Allison drew a breath and opened the book that was separate from the others. Each page was filled with tiny, neat handwriting; its form more a journal than a diary. There seemed to be no organized daily entries. Oriel had simply written her thoughts whenever she chose—jotting down the date and the time and then plunging straight into her text.

Allison's gaze slid over some of the private thoughts before relenting. She had no right! The woman was dead. Her privacy should be respected. She let the book slide back against the others.

Still, she continued to look at them. If she was ever going to understand the situation here, she had to understand Oriel. The real Oriel. Oriel in her own words, in her own thoughts... not bits and pieces of other people's impressions.

She reclaimed the books and found the first entry in the first volume and started to read:

I've always thought that keeping one of these things was idiotic, but the doctor seems to think it will do me some good. What would really do me some good is a liter of Stoli and a few uppers, but I don't think the good doctor would approve. In fact, I'm *sure* the good doctor wouldn't approve. So to appease him—he'll probably want to see this, just like he's wanted to put his nose into everything else in my life—I'll pretend to contemplate my life. "What is it you're running away from, Oriel?" Stupid question. "You can't find happiness in the bottom of a bottle." Oh, yeah? "You're sick, it's an illness." Sure it is. Sometimes—most of the time—I'm sick and tired of living! So for as much of the time as I can I try to get away from it.... Would Daddy, if he were here, be shocked? Would he be ashamed of the way his little girl has turned out? But you had your own ways of escaping, didn't you, Daddy? You thought I didn't know. But I did. Sometimes I even watched you. You thought Mummy didn't know, either, but she did. The joke's on you!

Allison continued to read, turning page after page, moving through time with the eyes of another. Seeing that with all her wealth, Oriel had not been a happy person. She was difficult and petty and enjoyed the control she had over people; yet she was also the frightened young woman that Paul remembered, needing love and understanding and nurturing. She had been in awe of her father and yet she was afraid of him, afraid that she was going to be like him...then doing just that.

Of the people who claimed to be her closest friends—those now present in this house—she showed both contempt and compassion. One day she would resolve to do all that she could to make their lives easier—give each what they wanted most, what her father had denied them. In the next entry she would be planning to hurt them. Every slight, every argument, every tear was recorded.

Was she afraid to set them free? Is that what had stopped her? Afraid that she would lose the only family she had ever known? She didn't say. Except she seemed to mistrust everyone, including, on occasion, Paul.

Who can I trust? No one. Not even Paul. I used to be able to, but he hates me now. He thinks I do everything wrong, just like everyone— Mary and I had a talk last night. She said that Paul sees through me, knows me for what I am. But Mary's a bitch! All she wants to do is protect that precious husband of hers. I'll find a way to punish— Paul is so sweet to me. I wish I could believe that he really cares. I need to believe that he— I need to believe that someone—

Her thoughts had rambled from that point, especially in her latter entries, which were almost unreadable. Broken sentences, broken thoughts. A broken life.

Allison let the last book slide slowly shut. She knew that she had been given a special privilege that few other people experience—a glimpse into the soul of another human being.

Without conscious thought, she got to her feet and walked to the tall wardrobe where she opened the twin doors and once again looked at the clothing. She felt so close to Oriel.

Her fingers trailed the dresses on their hangers.

Then she brought one down.

PAUL WAS STILL SMARTING from his earlier confrontation with Frank. Why did so many people think that it was their place to give him advice, when he didn't ask advice from anyone? And for Frank, of all people, to say what he had said: *It's not healthy to live in the past . . . in order to move forward, a person has to let go . . . hate only twists you . . . sometimes love does, too.*

Where did Frank come off giving advice? What did he know about love? About caring? Especially about loving and caring for Oriel.

Paul moved smartly through the hall, intent on going upstairs. He had been for a walk, a long walk. He hadn't trusted himself to sit at the same table with any of them. Especially her. And he still wasn't ready for conversation.

Evan Sargent stepped into the hall, blocking his way.

"I've just been on the phone to a contact in Florida," Evan said smugly. "He's going to fly to the Caribbean tomorrow morning, locate the convent and see if he can talk to this Sister Dominica."

"Is that supposed to frighten me?" Paul asked coolly.

"I just thought you'd like to know. In case you want to clear the matter up before the truth comes out."

"Evan, you wouldn't know the truth if it smacked you in the face."

Evan's smile disappeared. "And you think that you would? Oriel only put up with you because you were like a puppy jumping around her feet. You amused her. But even a puppy can become annoying."

"The same as a husband who cheats?"

Evan's face grew rigid. "You told her about that, didn't you? You just couldn't wait! You had to do it!"

"I told her nothing," Paul said. "I wouldn't hurt her like that."

"I don't believe you! You like nothing better than to cause trouble for all of us! Which is exactly what you're doing now...causing trouble. But I'm on to you, Paul. You're not going to get away with it! Not this time!"

Paul's voice slipped to a dangerous level. "Which will you miss more, Evan? Oriel...or her fortune?"

"Oriel, you fool!"

Paul smiled coldly. "Now it's my turn not to believe *you.*"

Evan's face grew red from anger. "No matter what you claim...this house is mine! And if you're not careful, Paul, I'm going to throw you out of it! You and that little impostor you brought with you!"

Paul didn't deign to answer. He pushed past his nemesis and walked determinedly to the stairs. He did not look back.

His steps were clipped as he started down the upstairs hall. Even though he hated Evan, he hadn't been the one to tell Oriel of her husband's philandering. Someone else could claim that tainted honor. One of the others. But he couldn't truthfully say that he wasn't pleased with part of the result: Evan had been banned from Oriel's bedchamber. For the rest of it, though, he wished that it hadn't happened. Oriel had become so brittle afterward.

As he came upon her set of rooms, he meant to move on, to go to his room. But his feet stopped of their own accord and his hand lifted to knock.

ALLISON STARED AT HERSELF in one of the long mirrors that decorated the inside of the wardrobe doors. The dress was soft, flowing, and lifted lightly from her legs when she twirled. The tiny bangles, sewn here and there, sparkled with silver-blue light. It was a party dress with low-cut bodice and paper-thin shoulder straps. Silver straps for shoes were a perfect match.

As she continued to preen before the mirror, she smiled. She felt like a fairy-tale princess, ready for a ball.

If she closed her eyes, could she pretend to *be* Oriel? She felt so close to her after reading her words....

A strangled sound caused her to whirl toward the source. Paul, his features contorted, his eyes lighted with black fire, stood just inside the doorway.

Allison's hand went to her throat. She looked down at the dress. She hadn't meant to do it. She hadn't planned...

"I'm sorry," she said quickly, in a hurry to apologize. "I didn't mean—" But she could get no further. His unnerving look dried her words.

He started to come toward her.

Allison tried appeasement, "I'll take it off. Just give me a minute and I'll..."

"Stay where you are." His words, though husky, held the sting of a whip.

Instinctively Allison looked for an escape route.

Paul stopped directly in front of her and for the space of a second, did nothing but look at her with burning eyes.

Allison was aware of the explosiveness of the situation. He was angry because she was wearing Oriel's dress. Possibly she had worn it the last time he had seen her. In his opinion, she had done the unforgivable. So she should try to save herself. Right? But she couldn't make herself move.

Why?

Because when he looked at her like that, everything inside of her melted. Because no matter the cost, she was willing to pay it—just to be close to him!

Emotion flooded through her. She didn't know what she felt for him. It didn't have a name. But she was drawn to him as she had been drawn to no other man. In spite of everything, in spite of their odd situation, he was her dark knight, her dark hero... Suddenly she didn't care anymore that he had caught her out—that he might be angry, that he might disapprove. Her feelings were much too elemental.

When he reached for her, Allison didn't hesitate. His features were so familiar to her, so dear.

Her body fitted perfectly against his. She could feel the strength of his muscles, the intimate, moist warmth of his skin, the rapid rise and fall of his chest. His eyes were like black diamonds glittering in their own darkness. And when he brought his mouth close, she quivered in anticipation. She was ready for his kiss.

But instead of aiming for her lips, his lips trailed along the curving line of her jaw, along her cheek, over her eyes and back down her neck before moving onto the sensitive curves of her breasts. Then, wrapping his fingers in her hair, he smothered a soft cry before fastening his mouth to hers in a kiss of such feeling, such passion, such longing, that Allison wasn't sure if she would survive.

She was aware of being lifted, of being carried. She whispered his name.

Soon she was on the bed, lost in the softness of the covers. One by one the books fell to the floor. But she was not alone. The long length of Paul's body was stretched out beside her, partially on top of her, pressing her down as he kissed her, touched her, murmured words of love and need.

Allison's heart took wing. Had he begun to feel for her what she was beginning to feel for him?

She cupped the sides of his face and looked deeply into those night-dark eyes—lost herself in those night-dark eyes. She loved him! Awareness came suddenly, without warning. She saw herself in those night-dark eyes...

And saw that *he* saw only Oriel.

Chapter Ten

Allison wanted to cry out in pain. In fact, she must have made some kind of sound, because her anguish reached into the depths of Paul's soul and he pulled back, halting all movement, suspending desire.

Allison wiggled beneath him, trying to push him off her, trying to push him away.

He didn't understand. "What is it?" he asked. "What's wrong? Did I hurt you?"

Allison continued to push away from him.

Slowly, in confusion, he let her go.

She was on her feet in two seconds, breathing hard, her hair disheveled, her eyes accusing.

He rolled away from the bed, striving for sanity in the midst of his insanity. "What happened? I wouldn't hurt you. I'd never hurt you! Oriel, I..."

"*I'm* not *Oriel!*" she hissed.

Paul blinked.

The dress that had once looked so beautiful was now asunder. Both straps were off her shoulders and for modesty's sake she quickly righted them.

Paul blinked again. "Oriel, I . . ." he began again only to be interrupted.

"Stop *calling* me that! I'm Allison. *Allison!*"

"I don't—"

"Allison Williams! Allison Williams! *Say it!*"

Paul took refuge in anger. It was much easier than facing unpleasant reality. "I *know* who you are!" he claimed heatedly. "And if you don't shut up, so will the rest of the house!"

She glared at him. "Have you thought that maybe I don't care?" She strove to collect her emotions. "What you're doing is *wrong,* Paul!"

He took a step forward. "You don't know what you're talking about!"

She backed away an equivalent pace. "Oh, but I do! I'm *Oriel,* remember? The wonderful Oriel! The saintly Oriel! The Oriel who can do no wrong! Well, you were wrong about that, too. Oriel wasn't near the person you thought she was. She was just as obnoxious as her father, pulling these people back and forth . . . playing God with them."

"Which one of them told you that?" he demanded.

Allison retrieved several of the slim volumes from the floor, holding them up. "Oriel told me, Paul. *She* told me. In her own words . . . in her own writing!" She thrust the books into his hands. "Read them! Read them and maybe then you'll see how mistaken you've been. Read how she planned a neat little trick for Dusty. You know how she owns the rights to his songs? Well, she came up with the idea of selling some of them. For commercial use! Knowing full well what it would do to Dusty, knowing that what little self-worth he has left is tied up in those early songs. She threatened him with humiliation... all to bring him back under her control when he looked to be slipping away. That's not the action of a saint, is it? And there are other instances, too... things she did to each of them." She gathered the remaining books and added them to the ones held limply in his hands.

Paul looked down. "I don't believe this," he said flatly.

Allison's features started to crumple, but she quickly regained control. "Read them," she said. "Each of them, each and every line. Maybe then you'll understand."

Paul stared at her.

Allison stared back, lifting her chin with as much dignity as she could muster.

He left without another word.

Once the door was closed behind him, Allison slid to the floor. Her emotions had taken a battering, spiking and then crashing. She had discovered love, only to have it turned away by a man who was still deeply into denial about another woman.

Hot tears spilled over her cheeks. All she wanted to do was go home.

ALLISON REMAINED WAKEFUL into the night, the sofa once again her bed. She couldn't bring herself to return to the real bed where Oriel had lain, where she and Paul had...

Allison groaned, her memories vivid.

She loved him! She could deny it, but it would do no good. Of all men, he was the one.

She had always held a romantic's view. Even during the darkest hours, when she had been depressed about her grandfather's condition, in the back of her mind she had clung to the hope that one day she would find the person she could love. He would love her, and with the two of them together, all problems would be surmountable.

And now here she was. Nothing had worked as she hoped. For one simple reason—how did she fight a ghost? Especially when she looked exactly like the ghost and was a constant reminder to Paul each time he looked at her.

Why, of all men, did it have to be him? she asked in misery. And why did it have to be now? At another time, in another place... possibly things could have worked out between them. But not now. Would it ever be possible for him to see her for herself? As Allison? Or would Oriel always get in the way?

Allison dropped her face into her hands. Once, she had been happy that she looked so much like Oriel because it meant money she needed. But that was before she had come to know Paul, to love him. Before looking like Oriel had come to be such a curse.

What was she going to do?

THE SLIM BOOK IN PAUL'S hands fell shut, his finger marking the last entry in the last volume. After a moment he slowly allowed the finger to slide loose. If it hadn't been for the fact that these books were written in Oriel's hand, he would have rejected the contents as fake. She wasn't manipulative! She didn't connive! But it *was* Oriel's writing! Tiny, neat, contained. And in her tiny, neat and contained writing she had shattered every illusion he ever held about her.

She could be as vicious as he had thought her sweet. As calculating as he had thought her innocent. And much more emotionally disturbed than he had ever imagined. She wrote things about people—including himself!—that he knew to be false.

Hers was a tortured soul. Tormented, ill, needing help, and yet at the same time pushing it away. She was as responsible for her own destruction as any addict. Frank wasn't at fault. He had even seen proof that Frank had tried to help her in his own wounded way.

But there *had* been another side to her. One he had witnessed himself. That's why he found it so hard to believe— He *knew* that she cared about people: children in need, people with handicaps. She contributed to many causes. But there were few hints at such gentleness of spirit within the pages of these books.

Paul carefully stacked the final journal on his bedside table. He hadn't wanted to read them, didn't like what he had seen, but he had felt compelled to finish. Now all he knew was a curious emptiness. No emotion, no feeling.

Then shortly feeling came rushing back, over-whelming with its power. Surge after surge of anger ground at him. It was all *her* fault! Why had she done this to him? She shouldn't have been reading them in the first place! She'd had no right!

Paul jerked to his feet and before he could think clearly, he was at her door, banging on it to be admitted.

ALLISON CURLED INTO HERSELF at the sudden noise, just as she curled further into herself when once again he didn't wait to be admitted.

At first he didn't see her. He went straight to the empty bed then into the open bathroom, anger breaking off him in waves.

Allison watched as he spun about. Their eyes met. Her breath caught in her throat.

"You had no right!" he grated menacingly. "What a person writes in their own private papers is not meant for anyone else to see. It means nothing. Nothing!"

Allison forced herself to speak. "She needed help."

"I tried!" he shouted.

"From a competent professional—one who could really help her, one she could trust!"

Paul's dark eyes blazed, then went deadly cold. "You're not qualified to judge, so don't even try. All we have is a few more days here. Then you can wash your hands of this entire affair. You won't have to think of Oriel or Magda ever again. In the meantime, stay out of her things. Don't touch anything. Nothing about Oriel concerns you!''

Once again tears threatened to fall. He was blaming her for what Oriel had done! ''It concerns me when you think that I'm her!'' she defended.

Paul stiffened. He knew exactly to what she was referring. ''You have my promise. It will never happen again.''

Allison's huge green eyes held his gaze, tears shimmering on her lashes. That was what she wanted to hear and yet it wasn't. She loved him!

A muscle twitched at the side of Paul's jaw. Then he swung away from her, unable to bear her look of injured reproach.

THE CARPET OF PAUL'S bedroom would have had a path worn into it if he hadn't eventually fallen into his bed, exhausted.

He could deny it all he wished, but the stack of thin books remained at his bedside and no matter how many times he looked at them, the words did not alter.

He could blame her; he *had* blamed her. But the principal wrong was Oriel's—for what she had done to all those people over the years. She was Damien's daughter, through and through. Her father had taught her well.

Still, he loved her and ached for the pain that she must have suffered. If only he had known! She hadn't wanted to follow in her father's footsteps. Page after page, she had fought against it. But being near these people, coming under their influence... They had been like leeches, knowing that their host was in terrible trouble but sucking her life's blood until nothing remained.

Again his anger resurfaced. But this time, instead of centering on the woman down the hall, it was directed against the others. If he had wanted to make them suffer before, this new awareness only reinforced that determination... because hating them gave him focus. Gave his life purpose. Without it...

Paul closed his eyes.

Without it... he was unsure of exactly who he was.

THE DARKEST HOURS of night loomed ahead of Allison like a void. Twice she had let him see that she loved him and twice he had rejected her because of his obsession with Oriel.

She knew that she could have him. All she had to do was immerse herself in Oriel once again. Pretend to be her instead of Magda. He might be angry at first, but his anger wouldn't last long. Not considering the happenings earlier in this room and on the trail. He loved Oriel... wanted her. And looking like her, being the "her" he desperately needed, would give Allison the upper hand.

She was tempted. Truly, she was tempted.

Take what you want, when you want, and don't worry about tomorrow... some people lived by that philosophy.

But not her. For too many years she'd had to look ahead to the consequences of each act, and she couldn't change her basic personality now.

If she did she might be happy for a time, but it wouldn't last. She couldn't *be* Oriel forever. Sometime in the future—the seeds were already planted— she would start to resent the fact that he didn't love her for herself.

She . . . Allison! The young woman with the grandfather who needed her, who relied upon her even though he had little awareness of his dependency. The grandfather she would never abandon.

Allison burrowed her cheek into the softness of her supporting arm and started to cry. She cried until she fell into an uneasy sleep.

"DID I HEAR SHOUTING in your wing of the house last night, Paul?" Roger LeBlanc asked, smiling smugly as he buttered a roll.

Allison didn't look up from her grapefruit. She had done all that she could with her makeup this morning, but there were still traces of puffiness around her eyes. If anyone looked closely, she knew they would see that she had cried.

Paul, seated across the table from her, smiled into the bright morning light of the solarium. "It must have been your imagination, Roger. It was as quiet as a tomb in our wing."

"I was just wondering. I didn't think you could possibly be shouting at our little nun here."

"She's not a nun. Not yet, at any rate."

Jennifer Clark swept languidly into the room, Jim following her. "Nun?" she said. "Did I hear some-one say something about a nun?" She threw a none-too-friendly glance at Allison before saying, "Oh! You mean Magda. Good heavens, dear. You look a little whacked. Have trouble sleeping last night?" Jennifer seated herself in the chair that Jim pulled out for her. "I did, too. I kept hearing voices. I couldn't under-stand what they were saying, but they didn't sound very friendly—particularly one of them."

Roger's smile grew more predatory as he waited for a second denial.

Paul was not disturbed. He poured cream into his cereal. "I wouldn't doubt that this place isn't haunted. Oriel's spirit can't be resting very easily, do you think? She probably came back from the grave to visit one of you."

"The voices came from your end of the house, dar-ling. Not ours."

"Are you sure?"

Jim had claimed his own seat across from his wife. He flapped open a section of newspaper. "Stop talk-ing about ghosts," he grumbled.

Paul said, "I read somewhere that only the guilty have anything to fear from ghosts. Do you think that explains why Magda and I didn't hear them?"

"Because you're so innocent?" Jennifer taunted. "Don't make me retch."

"I don't claim that. It's just that we never did anything to anger her."

"And *we* did?"

Paul took a sip of his orange juice. "Mmm. This is good."

"Don't change the subject."

"All right. Do you believe in ghosts, Roger? Oh, that's right. Of course you do. *Spencer's Way* has a ghost in it, doesn't it? The spirit of an old man who comes back to help his grandson through a hard time. But then he was a good ghost. The kind I'm thinking of is different. One who wants revenge."

Roger pretended to yawn. "I find this subject extremely tedious."

"That's because you've lost the spark for creativity, Roger. That's also why you're a has-been. Your decline has nothing to do with Oriel or with Damien. You were well on your way long before you met them. A one-film wonder, isn't that the term?"

"Stop talking about ghosts!" Jim shouted, pounding his fist on the glass-topped table, making the cups and saucers bounce.

Paul turned away from Roger's smoldering look. He smiled at Jim. "And what about you? From your reaction, I'd say you believe in the kind of ghost I'm talking about. The kind that doesn't rest until it's dealt with everyone who wronged it. Are you going to be able to sleep tonight, Jim? Is your conscience clear? If Oriel comes to confront you, will Spencer be able to look at her and tell her that you had no part in her death?"

"She died at the institute . . . in a fire, remember?" Jennifer drew Paul's attention from her husband, who had grown rather pale. "It was an accident."

"Was it?"

"Of course it was! It was investigated by the authorities and ruled an accident. Some kind of fault in the wiring. Are you telling us now that you don't believe that?"

"It was rather convenient. A lot of people stood to profit."

Jennifer flashed a quick look at Roger and her husband. "Are you accusing one of us of . . ."

"I'm accusing no one. I just said that it was convenient."

"You're insane, Paul."

Paul leaned back in his chair and smiled lazily, his attractive features seemingly relaxed. "I'll put the results of my inkblot test up against yours any day."

Jennifer sprang from her chair. She turned on her two companions. "How can you just sit there and take this? Why don't you *do* something? *Say* something? Am I the only one with enough guts to stand up to him?"

Roger stood up. "If anyone wants me, I'll be in the pool." He ignored Jennifer's incredulous look.

"Come on, honey," Jim urged. "Let's go for a walk." His wife's look turned to him. Jim explained tightly, "He's only trying to get a rise out of you."

"But you heard what he said!"

"I doubt he actually believes it."

"How do you know?"

To spite them, Paul continued to smile.

"Come on," Jim said, pulling tentatively on his wife's arm. "We'll have breakfast later."

Still wanting to spit fire, Jennifer let herself be drawn away.

Allison had sat quietly throughout the barbed exchanges, doing nothing to bring attention to herself—and she wanted that status to continue. But with only the two of them left in the large sunny room, she knew her wish was doomed.

Meeting him this morning had been the hardest thing she had ever had to do. She didn't know how he would react. Typically, he was withdrawn. He had come to her door, tapped on it once, motioned her ahead of him down the hall and not said a word until they were at the table, and that was to Roger, not to her.

She fussed with her grapefruit, having no intention of eating it. Tension crackled in the air, whether a leftover from the previous scene or a precursor of a scene to come, she didn't know.

She glanced at him. He was still sitting back in his chair; in place of his earlier taunting smile was a frown.

She cleared her throat. "Do you believe that?"

"What?"

"Do you believe that one of them could have...?"

He cut her off. "No! They're too stupid. Too afraid."

"Then why did you . . . ?"

He leaned forward. "We don't have much time left. Evan has an investigator flying to Marabu. He'll discover the truth soon."

"What will happen then?" she asked.

Paul shrugged.

"Aren't you worried?"

He didn't answer directly. After drinking the rest of his orange juice, he said, "I don't feel like facing the second wave quite yet. Are you finished?"

Allison abandoned her mangled fruit. She pushed away from the table in unison with Paul and accidentally their bodies touched. Both instantly shied away.

Allison's first instinct was to race from the room. Her second was to stay. She looked at Paul. This time, really looked at him. Even though he seemed exactly the same on the outside, inside she sensed a change. A deeper grief.

Her heart was pierced. "Paul—" she said softly, tentatively. "I'm sorry about what happened last night. I'm sorry you had to read those journals."

He went rigid. "Just keep quiet about the journals. Don't say anything."

"But . . ."

"Don't you understand? Nothing's changed!"

Allison looked away, her spirit heavy. Would nothing change the way he felt about Oriel?

Evan entered the room. At first he looked annoyed to see them, then his look changed to one of interest when he sensed that there was tension between them.

"Have I come at a bad time?" he asked with mock innocence.

Paul stood up. "Magda and I were just leaving."

"Oh?" Evan strolled to the serving table and lifted several lids. With slight interest he helped himself to scrambled eggs and toast. A young maid brought him coffee.

Paul put his hand at Allison's back and urged her toward the door.

Allison glanced back at Evan. He was watching them closely.

"I heard from my friend," he said, catching them just as they were about to step into the hall. "He's arrived in Barbados and is scheduled for an inter-island hop." He glanced at his watch. "He should be leaving right about now, actually, and arriving in Marabu in a couple of hours. I thought you might like to know."

"You should try your hand at reading television news, Evan," Paul scoffed. "You'd be good at it. When Magda makes her claim, you'll be needing something to fall back on."

Evan's movements stopped. "She's making a claim?"

Paul smiled. "Did I say that? I meant *if*. *If* Magda makes her claim."

Pressure on her back again urged Allison from the room.

Voices were coming toward them from around the corner of the hall. The people couldn't be seen yet, but they weren't far away.

"Don't let what Evan said worry you," Paul said quickly, close to her ear. "We still have time. Just keep up the act. Leave the rest to me."

Pressure was again exerted on her back. As they moved on, they met Mary LeBlanc, Dusty and Jean Anne. The two women were dressed for tennis. Paul would have gone by without stopping, but Jean Anne reached out to detain him.

"We were having a discussion, Paul," she said. She left her hand on his arm. "Mary said she wouldn't, I said she would, and Dusty— Well, you know Dusty. Sometimes he just can't make up his mind."

Paul waited impatiently. Jean Anne threw Allison a sly look, which made her brace for the worst.

"We were wondering if Magda would like to play tennis with us this morning. I know she doesn't have the proper attire, but surely she could look through a few drawers and find something of Oriel's to put on. We don't mind waiting."

A portion of Allison's tension ebbed. But not a lot. She didn't trust Jean Anne. And for good cause.

"I don't know," Paul said stiffly. "Why don't you ask her?"

Jean Anne smiled. "Because *you* seem to be the power behind the throne. I thought we'd just go direct...skip the middleman."

"You'll have to ask her," Paul repeated.

Jean Anne's gaze settled spitefully on Allison. She couldn't mask her hatred. "Well?" she demanded. "Can you answer, or do you have to check with Paul first? He's here. Ask him!"

Allison wanted to treat Jean Anne as she sometimes wanted to treat the nastiest customers—do some sort of violence to them! But just as with the customers, instead of resorting to savagery, she smiled sweetly and said, "Not this time, thanks."

"Do you know how to play?" Jean Anne persisted.

"A little."

"Then what's stopping you?"

Paul intervened. "Maybe it's your sweet personality, Jean Anne."

The woman jerked her hand away, as if suddenly stung by his touch. "Something else we've been wondering," she said, her tone growing even more unpleasant. "If she gets the money, what's she going to do with it? Give it to that convent she claims to be from?"

"If she wants to, yes," Paul said. "It would be her right. Just as it was Oriel's right to do what she wished with her inheritance. So maybe you should be nicer to her. Stay on her good side instead of ridiculing her. That is, if you're capable of such behavior."

"I was a better friend to Oriel than you think!" Jean Anne claimed. "She relied on me. She—" She touched the underside of her eye with one finger, as if brushing away a tear. "I was the one who convinced her to check into the institute this last time. I was the one who saw that her problem had gone too far.''

''Weren't you also the one who gave her the pills the first time? Weren't you hooked on them yourself?'' Paul used some of the information he had read in the journals.

Jean Anne blanched. She had to wonder how he had found out.

''That was a long time ago, Paul,'' she defended.

Mary and Dusty eased away until they stood a little apart.

''A very long time,'' Jean Anne repeated. ''I really tried to help her this time.''

''And she ended up dead.''

Jean Anne laughed, a forced sound that contained no merriment. ''Yes! Isn't that hysterical? There I was, trying to help her, and the damned place burns down!''

Paul didn't ease up on her. ''Then it finally looked as if you and Dusty were going to get the rights back to his songs. What were you going to do with them? Sell them for commercial use yourselves?''

Jean Anne's head snapped up. ''And what if we were? They're his. He wrote them. If anyone should have the money, he should!''

''And Oriel stood in the way.''

''We were in Oregon the night she died! We weren't anywhere near L.A.!''

''Do you have proof?''

Jean Anne looked at him as if he had struck her. Then, angrily, she struck back. The sound of her open hand hitting his cheek echoed through the hallway.

Allison caught her breath. The force of the blow had jerked Paul's head; the imprint showed white on his skin. At the corner of his mouth several drops of blood had started to gather.

He would not be diverted from his quest. "I'd still like to see your proof," he said.

Jean Anne drew back to slap him again, but Paul's hand shot out to arrest it.

"Dusty," he said tightly, his dark eyes glittering. "Come get your woman. Before I forget my manners."

Mary LeBlanc snickered, but when Paul swung round to face her, his look was enough to silence her.

Dusty rescued Jean Anne from Paul's grasp. She fought him, but after a moment accepted the comfort of his arms.

Paul reclaimed Allison's arm and walked stiffly away from the crowd. His cheek was a fiery red now, the drops of blood forming a thin line.

At the stairs they met Frank Alexander, who was coming down. He paused at the base. Even at this hour, he was wobbly. A grin spread over his features, lengthening his mustache.

"And what mischief have you been up to so early in the morning, my good man? Did you say the wrong thing to a lady? And which lady? Surely not our little Magda."

Paul started to push past him. "Get out of the way, Frank."

Frank smiled. "There's nothing to be ashamed of, Paul. Unless you reverted to debauchery. But somehow I can't see you doing that. Not our straitlaced, straight-arrow Paul." His eyes twinkled as he raised Allison's hand to his lips. He even winked at her. "But I won't insist that you tell me. Some things are best left unsaid." Then he started to move away, but tripped lightly over something invisible. "Ahh...I'd best find some strong coffee," he mused. "I must be in desperate need of it."

Allison had reached out to steady him. He smiled and patted her hand.

"An angel," he murmured. "No, a bird...a beautiful bird with iridescent wings and such magnificent green eyes that they capture a man's soul. Isn't that right, Paul?"

"You should go sleep it off, Frank," Paul suggested.

He met Paul's disdainful look and shook his head. *"The gifted know little of what they receive until they no longer have it.* I don't know who said that. Possibly me, in some play. But it's true, Paul. It's true." Then turning to Allison, he pleaded, "Come brighten my table, lovely bird. This philistine doesn't appreciate you."

Allison rejected the idea of being alone with Paul again, but neither did she want to face the others in the solarium. She smiled gently at Frank and suggested, "Another time, perhaps?"

Frank looked first at Paul, then at her, his eyes narrowing when he saw what Allison could do little to hide from a discerning eye. An expression of sadness passed over his features, then he forced a smile. "Of course. Another time. We immortals have forever—"

"Poetic fool," Paul complained as they started to climb the stairs, leaving Frank to make his way to the solarium as best he could. "If he'd put half as much effort into his plays as he does drinking, he'd have something."

"I wish I *were* Magda," Allison said softly.

"Why?"

"Because I'd back his special play."

Paul looked at her with puzzlement. "Why? You haven't even read it."

"Does it matter? It's his dream. Everyone's entitled to have a dream come true."

Paul's expression became unreadable. When he dropped her at her door, he said tersely, "Give them an hour, then do what you want. Go for a walk or something. But don't wander far."

Allison nodded. She started to slip through her door but hesitated. "Paul?" she called softly, halting his retreat. "Are you sure you don't believe that one of them...harmed...Oriel?"

Paul's frown was quick. "No," he said. "I don't." But his previous conviction just wasn't there anymore. He now seemed a little uncertain.

He retained his frown as he walked away.

Allison curled onto the sofa after slipping off her shoes.

Life in this house was so alien. More like an Agatha Christie novel than the American Dream. Only there hadn't been an actual murder yet . . . had there?

Chapter Eleven

Why hadn't the idea occurred to him before? He had blamed them for everything else, but he had missed the one possibility that now seemed most obvious: *had one of them killed Oriel?* The thought, like a cold wind, shuddered through the recesses of Paul's mind.

At first the notion seemed impossible. He had known most of these people for years, some from as far back as his arrival at the Woodrich home as a boy. He didn't like them; he had never liked them. But murder?

Paul raked a hand through his hair. Life was becoming more surreal by the minute. *Could* one of them have done it? Had one of them reached a point of such desperation? He had assured Allison that he didn't believe any of them brave enough to do it—it did take a certain amount of fearlessness, didn't it, to end another's life? But if either reward or relief was so great, what would have kept one of them from . . .

He didn't want to believe it—a reaction that shocked him. For Oriel's sake, for his sake, for the sake of everyone involved, he hoped that he was wrong. It was one thing to blame them for hounding Oriel to her death, and quite another to suspect that one of them had actually killed her! He didn't want to take that step. He didn't want to look inside himself and see that he could believe it.

Reading Oriel's journals had shaken him. She had always been the standard by which he judged other women. Had he been blind? Or had she reserved a side of herself only for him—because it was only through his eyes that she could see the good that remained in her?

Paul's gaze dropped to the journals. If he had been wrong about Oriel, could he also be wrong about everything else?

ALLISON LEFT THE HOUSE by way of the front terrace. On that course she wouldn't be seen by any of the other guests using the facilities in the backyard. She could have a few short minutes of peace with nature, away from all the others. Away from tension and suspicion.

The clean, pure air welcomed her, as did the warming rays of the sun as it shone through the trees and dappled the pathway. She wanted to see the lake. They would be leaving the area in a few days, possibly sooner, if Evan's detective was able to breach the security of the convent. She did not have much time left.

Did she wish that she had never agreed to play the part of Magda? She didn't know. The money would be of such great help to her grandfather and herself. But she had paid a giant price. Her emotions had been assaulted by everyone; but especially by Paul, who didn't even know that he was hurting her because he was hurting so desperately himself. Yet all of them were hurting, in their own individual ways, from their own individual weaknesses.

Allison's thoughts returned to Paul. What would happen to him once they left this house? After this week she probably would never see him again, unless he happened into the restaurant during one of her shifts, which was doubtful.

And herself? She had never thought much about the way she looked. Now she wondered if ever again she would be able to look into a mirror without seeing another image in the background . . . the woman who had come before her.

Moving quickly through the meadow, unwilling to dwell upon the future or the immediate past, she soon broke through the line of trees that ringed the lake and stood at the water's edge.

From her position on an out-thrusting ledge, the view was excellent. The blue water of the lake matched exactly the blue of the sky, its great depth seemingly as limitless. Like a jewel it shone in its mountainous setting, rugged and breathtaking and unending. It felt good to see something that had existed through time, and would continue to exist no matter what man did. Huge rocks dotted the shoreline beneath Allison's feet and as she looked down, she saw that the path contin-

ued in a rather haphazard way from time-worn rock
to time-worn rock. Great cracks were evident in some
of the boulders, a threat that one day they would sur-
render to gravity and disperse. But not yet.

Allison set off along the rugged descent. There was
some danger, but she had good balance. And as long
as she concentrated on what she was doing... Stepping carefully from one rock to another, she tried to
ignore the great crevices under which water sometimes gurgled.

The last rock jutted into the lake, more of a short
precipice than a natural jetty. It was as if the entire
jumbled mess had at one time been part of some
higher ledge that had given way. She stood on the last
flat surface. A light wind whipped her hair, just as it
whipped the water into glittering, dancing peaks a
distance from her feet. Colors shifted and
changed... greens and golds and blues. A combina-
tion. A speedboat cut a line through the middle of the
lake, soon followed by another. Even the muted roar
of a chain saw being used on the nearby bank seemed
somehow to fit in.

Allison smiled and lifted her arms to the sun, then
dropped them in a wide circle. She had come to Lake
Tahoe with her father once, when she was a very
young child. She spent most of her time in a hotel
room then, waiting for her father to tire of the gam-
bling casinos, but he had taken a few minutes one
morning to bring her to the lake. To her child's eyes,
it seemed like a great inland sea. She had never for-

gotten it and always wanted to come back. She was not disappointed.

A bird, soaring on a wind current, caught her attention. From her perspective far below, it looked to be hanging motionless in the sky. Then it flapped its wings, making a minute adjustment, and returned to its previous motionlessness. It was riding on a wind current, edging sideways bit by bit.

Allison lifted a hand to shade her eyes so that she could continue to watch the bird against the brightness of the sky. She wondered how much longer it would continue to glide... when suddenly from the rear a blow hit her squarely on the head. Almost simultaneously another blow fell between her shoulder blades, knocking the breath from her lungs. Then she felt herself stagger and pitch forward....

Allison battled back to consciousness as icy water closed over her head. With instinctive need she began to struggle, kicking her feet, thrashing her arms. She hit something hard... rocks, gravel. Her skirt tangled about her legs. Finally, gathering her senses, she realized that the water wasn't deep. That if she just pushed upward...

Her head broke the surface a second later. She gasped for air, blinking, trying to see. Water choked her. She coughed. She coughed again.

Numbing coldness slowed her movements as she crawled toward the nearest jumbled rocks. She couldn't understand what had happened! One moment she was enjoying the view, the next she was struggling for her life!

After pushing shakily to her feet, her head started to swirl. When the freshening breeze hit her, she began to shake. Her dress clung to her like a second skin, her hair streamed down her neck and over her face. She swept some wet strands back with a quivering hand. Her teeth started to chatter.

She didn't understand!

Then she remembered the blows—the surprise of them, the pain. Now that she thought about them, both areas stung. Someone had hit her? Someone had knocked her into the water? She couldn't believe it. Who?

Then memory again supplied an answer and Allison shuddered deep within her being, not merely from the cold.

Looking around, she realized that she had to get out of there. What if her attacker was still around? What if they tried again? For a moment she panicked. Then rationality resurfaced. What she had experienced was more a hit-and-run type of move, not a direct confrontation. If the person who had done it had stayed to watch, they were doing it from a safe distance. They wouldn't want to be caught anywhere near if their plan proved successful.

A familiar voice, quoting Shakespeare with a slightly drunken air, suddenly floated to her ears.

Obeying instinct, Allison flattened against the nearest large rock, which happened to be the one she had been standing on.

Even though she was freezing, she was afraid to ask for help. What if Frank was the one who had assaulted her?

Frank continued his soliloquy, giving no indication that he knew she was there.

Allison waited, hopeful that he would leave. Finally she could stand it no longer. "Frank!" she called.

His words immediately halted.

"Frank," she repeated. "Down here!"

His head popped over the edge of the rock, his eyes widening at her state. "Good God, girl! What's happened to you?"

Frank *couldn't* have been the one who hit her. He couldn't have been and now look so concerned.

"I—I...fell. Frank, do you think you can help me up?"

He hesitated. "Do you have an idea?"

The rock was much too smooth for Allison to climb. So, too, were most of the others nearby. She contemplated her choices. She could barely feel her feet anymore. She *had* to get out of the water.

"Over there," she said, pointing to a cleft in the rocks near the shoreline, close to the start-up of the real path. From this vantage point, the strewn rocks seemed to broaden and flatten as they lifted. It looked to be her surest bet.

"Are you sure you can make it?" Frank asked, concerned.

"I'll make it," Allison said resolutely.

"Should I find a rope or something...or better yet, get somebody else? I'm not very good at being a hero."

"I'm freezing, Frank! I don't have time to wait!" She didn't tell him that she didn't trust any of the others. Or that she didn't want Paul to find out yet.

"All right," he called. "I'll meet you there...if I don't end up falling in myself."

"Be careful!" she called, alarmed.

"*Careful* is my middle name...when I haven't been indulging. And I'm sorry to say that I have been. Indulging, that is. So it makes this all the more difficult."

"If you got out this far, you can get back," she encouraged.

"I wasn't thinking about it then."

"Frank!" She let her teeth chatter loudly for emphasis.

"All right. I'm going!"

Allison hunched her shoulders and held onto her arms. Her entire body seemed to be quaking now. From shock, from the cold. She moved her feet only with the greatest of will. But she made it to the flatter rocks and found Frank waiting for her. He leaned forward, extending his hand. She struggled, slipping occasionally, bashing her shin, twisting her ankle, scraping her knees and fingertips. But finally she was able to reach his hand and felt his fingers close firmly around her own.

Once she reached safety, Allison collapsed. Frank removed his jacket and wrapped it around her shoulders. She pushed clinging tendrils of hair away from her face and thanked him.

"Your hands are bleeding," he said, shocked.

"I'll get blood on your jacket!" She tried to remove it.

"Never mind about that. Your legs are scraped, too. Can you walk? I'd offer to carry you, but we'd never make it."

Allison drew a deep breath and as soon as she was able stood up with Frank's help. When she swayed slightly, he transferred his arm to her waist.

"The blind leading the blind," he murmured, cracking a wry smile as they started off. "Maybe between the two of us, we'll find home port."

Allison smiled through chattering teeth. She didn't think she'd ever get warm again.

HER RETURN TO THE HOUSE caused a sensation. Frank insisted on taking her along the shortest route, which meant the rear terrace where most of the others were gathered.

"Magda's had an accident!" he called when they had barely emerged from the pathway.

Dusty and Jean Anne and Roger looked up. They were nearest, lounging around the pool. Dusty jumped up and jogged toward them, Roger quickly following.

"What happened?" Dusty asked as he came up to them, his face paling at the sight of blood.

"She fell in the lake," Frank puffed.

"Holy—"

"Should we call a doctor?" Roger asked a second later.

"No!" Allison cried. "I'm not hurt."

"You don't sound too good, or look it. I think we should call someone."

"Get some blankets," Dusty said, taking her free arm to drape over his shoulders.

At that moment Paul ran up to them, his face showing little emotion but his eyes hollow with shock. His gaze ran swiftly over her, checking how badly she was hurt.

"What happened?" he demanded, his voice razor-sharp.

"She fell in the lake," Frank replied.

"Are you all right?" he asked. "Are you hurt?"

Frank had intimated that the house was a safe harbor. All Allison wanted to do was throw herself in Paul's arms and burst into tears, telling him of her fear, receiving his assurance. Because *he* was her safe harbor. Only with him would she be safe...for the rest of her life. Instead she answered huskily, "No, I'm not hurt."

Paul saw the intention of the other two men to walk side by side with her to the terrace. He stepped forward, saying brusquely, "I'll take her." Then he swept her into his arms, uncaring that his clothing would be damaged, and started for the house. The others fell into step at the rear.

"Just luck," Allison heard Frank explain when Dusty asked how he had found her. "Just luck," he said again when Evan, meeting them on the terrace, asked the same thing.

So many pairs of eyes probed her face and her form that Allison wanted to hide. Most were curious or concerned, but one pair, she knew, had to conceal disappointment. Allison didn't know which.

"Call Dr. Matthews," Paul directed.

"No," Allison tried again. "Please—"

"Do it!" Paul snapped. He started indoors.

"Would you like me to help?" Jennifer offered.

Paul felt Allison's immediate stiffening even in the midst of her shivering. He shook his head.

"I'll send up Mrs. Wainwright," Evan said.

This offer Paul did not refuse. "Tell her to bring some hot tea."

He didn't wait any longer. As they started up the stairs, Allison let her head loll against his shoulder. She felt as if she was floating. But she wasn't afraid, because the strong arms that supported her were so welcome.

The rest of the trip to the suite was accomplished in something of a haze. Paul sat her on the sofa and went in search of a blanket. He found one in the closet where Allison's small array of dresses were hung. He slipped it around her shoulders, wrapping her up tightly, trying to stop the quivering that she couldn't control.

"P-Paul—" she tried to say.

He stopped her. "We'll talk later. Right now, I'm going to run a bath. We've got to warm you. Are you sure you're not injured?"

Allison nodded.

He walked briskly into the bathroom and soon the spray of water could be heard rushing into the tub. Several moments later he returned.

He helped Allison to her feet. "Would you like me to carry you?"

She would! But she shook her head.

When she stood up, he walked closely at her side, his arm giving support. Inside the bathroom, Allison could see that he had been busy. Two giant white towels were folded on a stand, and he had poured a little of Oriel's favorite bath oil into the water. The aroma wafted delicately upon the air.

He helped rid her of the blanket, then of Frank's jacket, then at the next step, he hesitated.

"I can do it," Allison choked. She lifted her hands to the buttons that fronted her bodice. But they shook so badly, it was soon painfully apparent that she couldn't undo them.

With a poker face, Paul swept her hands away and carefully undid the buttons himself.

Allison blushed at her helplessness. Her blushed deepened as he slid the dress from her shoulders and it fell into a wet heap at her feet.

"Turn round," he murmured.

Allison couldn't meet his eyes. She kept her gaze fastened firmly on the plush carpeting as she turned her back. His fingers felt like fire on her cold skin. Her bra was unhooked in the space of a second.

"Think you can manage from here?" he asked. "Can you get in the tub?"

Allison made the mistake of looking into the bronze mirrors that backed the bath. In them she saw Paul standing tall and heartbreakingly handsome directly behind her. Her coloring was like a flame to his darkness. She caught her breath. His gaze lifted, met hers . . . held. Then quickly it was pulled away.

"Yes," Allison choked, looking away as well. Tears filled her eyes. Tears of weakness, of lost hope.

He moved away. "I'll be in the bedroom. Call if you need me."

Allison waited for the door to close, but he didn't pull it to. So that he could hear her more easily if she called? She was wholly aware of his nearness as she finished undressing and stepped into the water. At first it felt hot to her abused skin, stung the cuts. Then, as she immersed herself and the bath began to work its magic, the water turned out to be merely warm. In fact, as it transferred its heat to her, she had to add more warm water from time to time in order not to become cold again.

The flowery fragrance of the bath oil extended to Oriel's shampoo and Allison had no compunction about using it. If only she could wash away the memory of being pushed off the rock as easily as she washed her hair.

She continued to add more warm water until finally she stopped shaking and then forced herself to step out.

After drying herself with one fluffy white towel, she wrapped the second, like a sarong, about her slender body. Her fresh clothes were all in the other room.

She pulled the door open. Paul was waiting on the sofa. He looked up when he realized that she was in the room; his face was impassive.

"Mrs. Wainwright brought soup and tea," he said gruffly. "I think you should have some, even if you don't want it. You're warm now, but we want to keep you warm."

Allison stepped lightly to the bed. It was the only place left for her to sit. And she truly didn't feel strong enough to stand. Not at the moment at any rate. Holding the towel carefully about herself, she climbed onto the softness.

The bed tray was sitting on the small round table in front of the sofa. Paul collected it and motioned for her to scoot back against the pillows before adjusting the tray expertly across her legs.

Allison obediently ate the chicken soup and drank a cup of hot tea, the warmth spreading throughout her system, starting with a tingling in her tummy, then moving on to her fingers and toes and bringing a light flush to her cheeks.

Paul poured her a second cup of tea then sat carefully on the foot of the bed.

"Feel better?" he asked, smiling slightly.

Allison's heart skipped a beat at that smile. She nodded.

"The doctor is on his way. Evan caught him just as he was about to leave the hospital. It shouldn't be long now."

"But I'm fine! Nothing's broken, nothing's hurt, except for a few scratches. And they're not bad enough to take up a doctor's time."

"I'd still feel better if he examined you. So would everyone else."

Allison wiggled in place. "I doubt that," she murmured.

"Your fall has shaken them," he said.

"Only because it didn't kill me!"

Paul's eyes narrowed. "What makes you say that?"

Allison didn't want to tell him. He had already been through so much. But he had to know. "Someone pushed me, Paul! They hit my head, then my back. I didn't just fall into the water. It wasn't an accident!" When he said nothing, Allison found the bump on the back of her head and leaned forward, almost unsettling the tray. "Feel it!" she cried. "It's right here!"

Paul moved the tray back to the table, then came to stand next to her. Allison took his hand and guided his fingers to the tender bump.

"See?" she said. "I felt both hits, then I fell forward. The next thing I knew I was in the water. If I hadn't come to when I did..." She let the rest hang in the air.

His hand moved away.

"It wasn't deep," she continued, trying to talk herself away from the idea that she herself had just raised. Thinking otherwise frightened her. "And I guess I wasn't hit all that hard, because I did wake up right away. But whoever did it wanted to hurt me . . . at the very least!"

"And you suspect one of them?"

"Wouldn't you?"

Paul thrust his hands into his pockets and rocked back on his heels. His back was ramrod straight. His eyes, as they roamed over her face, reflected forced control.

"As I said, the doctor will be here shortly. I'll show him up myself."

"But what about . . . ?"

"Would you like me to find you a gown?"

Allison pointed to the closet. She didn't know why he was reacting so coolly to her accident. "My things are in there," she said.

He came out with a simple pink gown that should have clashed violently with her hair but somehow didn't. He draped it over the end of the bed.

"I'll be back shortly," he said. "In the meantime, get some rest."

As he walked away, Allison called, "Paul?" There was intense vulnerability in her tone but she could do nothing about it. "You do believe me . . . don't you?"

Paul lost the rhythm of his steps. Partially turning, he said simply, "Yes. I believe you."

Chapter Twelve

"How is she?" Frank asked anxiously. He had been hovering outside the door to Oriel's suite, waiting for Paul to come out.

"She'll live," Paul said tersely.

Frank was pale and slightly disheveled, not at all his usual glib self. "I couldn't believe it when I heard her call. I was at the end of the trail, standing on the rocks, then this voice came from below me in the water. It was quite... sobering."

"But not enough to keep you that way." The smell of alcohol was fresh on Frank's breath.

"Hey! I only had one drink. And I needed it! I'd just had quite a shock!"

Paul started to push past him.

"When can I see her?" Frank asked, grabbing on. "Right now? Just for a minute?"

Paul's dark eyes glimmered. "Don't you think she's been through enough for one day?"

"All I want to do is talk to her!"

"She's resting."

"You don't own her, Paul!"

"I brought her here."

"That still doesn't give you the right to make decisions for her."

"It makes her my responsibility!"

Frank paused. "Aren't you coming to that idea just a little late?"

The thrust hurt. It hit much closer to home than Paul was prepared for. "I don't know what you mean," he denied.

Frank's mustache quivered. "Oh, I have a feeling that you do. In the meantime, you're probably right to keep up your guard...what with all the piranhas swimming around."

Paul shifted slightly, dislodging Frank's restraining hand. "And what about you? You don't consider yourself a piranha?"

"Who, me? Oh, no. I see myself more as a sleek eel, cutting through the water without making a ripple."

"Moray?" Paul hazarded.

Frank laughed. "Nothing that fierce, I'm afraid. Definitely nothing that fierce."

When Paul pulled away again, Frank didn't stop him.

PAUL WAITED IN THE ROOM nearest the front door, where he could keep an eye and ear tuned to Allison's door upstairs and also be aware of when the doctor arrived. To anyone watching, he might have looked calm and collected. Inside himself, he was anything but. Emotion tumbled through him, a volley of painful thoughts.

He still didn't want to believe it, but he couldn't ignore what had just occurred—someone had tried to kill her! The same someone who had killed Oriel? It wouldn't take a leap of logic to recognize that if someone had wanted to eliminate Oriel, that same someone would have no compunction about removing another threat. And they had almost succeeded! If Allison had been hit just a little harder...

Paul shuddered at the idea of her body floating facedown in the shallows....

And it would be his fault! He had been playing a dangerous game here. One he hadn't given proper consideration to. He had cared for nothing except revenge. Certainly not the young woman he had hired for the part. All that had mattered to him was her amazing physical resemblance to Oriel, and the use he could put it to.

Unthinking, uncaring, he had bribed her away from her everyday life, brought her to this place and offered her like a sacrificial lamb upon the altar of his obsession. He had even advised her to go for a walk once he had begun to suspect...

Paul groaned and raked a hand through his hair. He had told Frank that she was his responsibility and he was right. More right than he had first wanted to admit. When he had seen her limping up the path, his heart had dropped to his toes!

Randall, in his wisdom, had warned him that one day he might come to regret his actions, but he had been too stubborn to listen.

He had been too stubborn to listen about a lot of things. Too absorbed.

But he couldn't go back now and change things. It was too late. All he could do was go forward.

THE DOCTOR pronounced Allison fit after examining her. "If you have nothing to get out of bed for, stay put. Your body's had a shock, let it rest...and keep warm."

Neither Allison nor Paul corrected the doctor's assumption that she had hit her head in the fall.

Paul returned to her room after seeing the doctor to his car. Looking at her, tucked safely beneath the covers, the delicate pink of her gown adding to the flush of her cheeks, he said, "He thinks you're lucky. He doesn't know quite how lucky."

"Somehow it doesn't seem real," she murmured softly.

Paul paced restlessly beside her bed before stopping to ask, "Do you have any idea who did it?"

She shook her head.

"Didn't you hear the person coming? A footstep? Anything?"

"Someone was cutting wood with a chain saw. I didn't hear anything else. I was looking at a bird, then the next thing I knew—"

"Could it have been someone else? A stranger?"

Allison hesitated. "It could have."

"But you don't believe that."

Allison shook her head. "It would be too much of a coincidence."

"Could it have been Frank? He seemed to show up right away."

"No."

"Why deny it so quickly? It could as easily be him as another."

"Not Frank."

His expression darkened. "He's got just as much to lose as anyone else. He could have come up behind you, hit you, hidden, then come back to take a look."

Allison continued to shake her head. "Not Frank. No. Not him!"

"Why are you defending him?" he charged, his frustration growing. "He's certainly no saint!"

"Because I think you're concentrating on him too much! And you're doing it because you hold a grudge. Because you loved Oriel and you can't stand the idea that he actually won her. If only you'd . . ."

"Stop trying to analyze everything so much! These people! This situation! Me! Everything's much more complicated than you think. Frank's smart. He knows how to play you. Pretty soon you'll be telling him everything!"

"And would that be such a terrible thing? Then it would be over!"

It wouldn't be over until he had confronted them, Paul knew; seen for himself the actual truth about Oriel's death.

"Just let me take care of it," he directed. "I'll decide what we're going to do and when."

"But it concerns me now!"

"What do you want?" he jeered. "Hazardous-duty pay?"

"Money isn't the answer to everything!" she denied, hurt.

"It seems to be with you!"

Allison recoiled as if he had hit her, and a muscle in Paul's cheek jerked. He hadn't meant that! Once he might have, but not now. He wasn't sure of anything anymore, except that he was angry and frustrated...and afraid. For her. He wanted nothing more than to spirit her out of this house and take her back to San Francisco. But if they left, so might the person responsible. And then he would never know.

Allison raised tear-filled eyes, her expression bruised. She blurted out, "If you must know, every penny I've taken from you is for my grandfather! He's ill. If I can't get enough money together, he'll have to go to a charity nursing home. And I'd do anything not to have to do that!"

"Even risk your life?" Paul was shaken. She had spoken about her grandfather once before, but as with everything else he had not believed her.

Allison looked away. "No," she said tightly. "Not that. Because if I'm not around, he'll have to leave our home anyway. When I agreed to do this job, you never told me that I'd be in danger. You're a selfish man, Paul Sullivan. You won't stop at anything to get what you want. And you don't care who you hurt. Exactly what makes you any different from the rest of them?''

Paul's heart skipped a beat.

He could give her no answer...because he had none.

ALLISON CRIED SILENTLY for most of an hour. She cried without making a sound, because Paul had stretched out on the nearby sofa after telling her that he wasn't going to leave her alone.

He had said nothing after her outburst, done nothing to defend himself.

She hadn't meant to go that far! She didn't really blame him for what had happened to her. But after the doctor left, she had wanted to do something to challenge him. To shake his firmly held convictions. He still seemed so intent on playing out his hand when he knew perfectly well that one of them was dangerous.

Allison cried for herself and for him. She cried herself to sleep.

SOMEONE SHOOK her shoulder. Shook it again.

Allison fought against the grogginess of sleep. Weak moonlight filtered through the curtain sheers, making the person only a form. Moonlight? It was night?

It took another moment for her to realize that the person standing over her was not Paul. Drawing a startled breath, her eyes wide with fright, she started to scream. Then a voice she associated with friend-ship reached her consciousness.

"Allison? Allison, honey? It's Randall. Come on . . . wake up."

"Randall?" she questioned fuzzily. "What are you doing here? What time is it?"

He sat down on the edge of the bed. "It's a little after three. I have some bad news. It's your grand-father. He's in the hospital. He's had another stroke."

As his words registered, Allison tried to struggle out of bed. She wanted to get dressed and get out of there, but Randall was in the way.

"Now, don't get in a dither," he continued calmly. "Right now he's holding his own. The nurse you hired called me a little before midnight. They'd just settled him in intensive care. When I got into Tahoe, I checked with her again. His condition is the same."

"I have to go to him!" Allison breathed.

"That's what I'm here for," Randall said warmly. "To take you back. Paul is downstairs getting some coffee for you."

Automatically Allison checked the sofa. It was empty. All through the time she had been asleep, she had been reassured by the idea of Paul's nearness. Now that she needed his reassurance again, he was gone.

"He knows?" she asked.

Randall nodded. "Do you need any help getting your things together?"

Allison shook her head. Nothing seemed real to her at this moment. Nothing had truly seemed real since yesterday, before her fall. Events were unfolding at amazing speed, but somehow they seemed in slow motion. Could this be a dream, too? A trick her mind was playing on her?

She reached out to touch Randall's hand and encountered the substance of flesh.

Randall understood. "I'm real, I'm afraid."

The door opened. Allison's hand jerked away, a flush rushing into her cheeks. She didn't want Paul to think... Then her flush spread even more in confusion.

Paul came to stand directly beside them. Randall switched on the nearest lamp. Paul was carrying a tray with several cups of steaming coffee. "It's instant. It's all I could find."

His eyes swept quickly over her, but she could read nothing in them. No concern, no compassion.

"There's no need for her to come back," he said, speaking directly to Randall as he found a place for the tray. "We've already accomplished what we wanted."

"In three days?" Randall frowned. "That was quick work."

"The situation moved fast."

Allison got unsteadily to her feet, her bruises and cuts protesting movement. Both Paul and Randall reached out to steady her, but Randall, who was closest, got to her first.

Allison tried to smile. She wasn't very successful. "I'll... get changed and get my things." Her gaze fell on Paul, hoping for some show of emotion. "I'm sorry to have to leave like this."

"It's for the best," he said. His voice was as cold as when she had first met him. He didn't care! she concluded painfully. He even seemed relieved that she was going!

Allison worked desperately to hide her injured feelings; but once she was in the bathroom, she leaned against a marbled wall and allowed some of the hidden tears to find release. Her grandfather was perilously ill, the man she had come to love didn't love her in return— In fact, he was unable to even see her as a person. To him, she was merely an image. One that could be erased as easily as it had been created.

The low exchange of voices in the next room slowly impinged on her sorrow. Drying her tears, she dressed quickly and presented herself, catching the tail end of what Paul had been saying, "... cover for her. They won't be able to say anything. Not after what happened."

Randall's back was to her. "I'll watch out for her in the city, just in case."

Paul caught sight of Allison and nudged his friend. Randall turned, giving a bright, encouraging smile in hope of cloaking what might have been overheard. "Quick work!" he said.

Allison looked at both men steadily. "I don't want anyone watching out for me. When I'm through with this place, I want to forget it!"

Paul reached into his pocket and held out a check. "Payment in full. I realize that this isn't cash, but I think you know I'm good for it."

What Allison really wanted to do was scream: *What about the others? What are you going to do about them? What are you going to say? What are you going to do when I leave? Don't put yourself in danger!*

"I don't want it," she said stiffly.

"Take it. You've earned it."

Randall slipped the check from between his friend's fingers and thrust it into Allison's hand. "There. That's done. Now let's go!"

Allison hurried to the closet and threw her clothes into the suitcase Paul had purchased, uncaring that they were jumbled.

When she was finished, she faced the two men. "I'm ready," she said.

Paul gave no sign that he had even heard. Randall took the case from her saying, "I made good time on the way here. We shouldn't have any problem getting back. It's still early."

Allison nodded. She continued to look at Paul. His eyes were like the darkest obsidian, impenetrable.

Then in the first thing of a personal nature that he had ever said to her, he murmured, "I hope your grandfather's health improves."

Just like that. Like a politely concerned stranger. As if the intimate episodes had never passed between them. She was no longer the person playing the role of Magda, who also reminded him of Oriel. She was merely Allison. A woman who had touched his life for a brief moment and now that moment was over.

Allison could think of nothing to say. This truly was the last time she would see him.

She turned to walk through the door, leaving for the last time the luxurious suite that had belonged to the woman who claimed him as firmly in death as she ever had in life.

In the car, as the headlights cut a wide swath through the darkness, Randall turned to look at her, concern in his steady gray eyes. Periodically a tear would slide down her cheek and she would wipe it away. But he never questioned her. He merely offered her the support of his hand, which Allison mutely accepted.

PAUL STOOD AT ONE of the long windows opening onto the front terrace and watched them drive away, his emotions pulling him back and forth. He didn't know what to think of her...or of the way he felt about her. Everything was so mixed up.

He was still so enmeshed in his feelings for Oriel, in the love that he had felt for her. He had worshiped her! Blindly, it seemed. But now that he knew her faults, did that lessen the intensity of his caring?

Paul went slowly back upstairs and stretched out on his undisturbed bed. He lay on the top cover and stared at the darkened ceiling.

He had done the right thing, hadn't he? Sending Allison away could be the equivalent of saving her life. He had no idea what he would be dealing with here in the future. He would have more flexibility without having to worry about her. She had served her purpose; she was no longer needed....

But when he had said as much in her presence, she looked stricken. He was sure that she had tried to hide it, but he had seen. So had Randall.

Randall was a good friend. The best of friends. And now he was extending his friendship to Allison.

Paul continued to stare at the ceiling.

Like him, Randall was a bachelor. There had been several women in his friend's life, but nothing serious. Until now? Was Randall befriending Allison to help him? Or to help his own cause?

Paul moved restively. Why should he care if he was? It was a free country, wasn't it? Randall could be interested in whomever he wished. Unlike himself, he didn't have any hang-ups from the past to contend with. Or slips of behavior.

Paul's cheeks darkened slowly as he remembered what he had done. He rarely ever lost control, but with her he had repeatedly. His feelings had run away with him. His love— His need— At the time it had felt as if he were falling in love with Oriel all over again.... He was able to touch her, to see her, to make love to her.... Only, was it Oriel with whom he was falling in love?

"Allison." Paul said the name softly, tentatively, hearing it spoken for the first time on his own lips. Then he groaned in misery as he covered his face.

Chapter Thirteen

Paul wanted to be done with it. He wanted to be done with *them*. So much of his life had revolved around them and their problems. Almost twenty-four years. He wanted it to be over!

If one of them had murdered Oriel, he wanted to discover who that person was and have him prosecuted. If one of them had tried to harm Allison, he wanted that known as well.

The games he had indulged himself with in the past were over. In this final confrontation, he was determined to win.

PAUL WAITED UNTIL LUNCH to go downstairs. As he planned, they were all in the dining room, seated at the table, just as they had been when he and Allison had first accosted them. Only two places were empty.

Evan looked at him crossly when he didn't immediately claim his seat. "Oh for heaven's sake, Paul, sit down! I can't eat with you hovering. And where's the girl? All she had was a little tumble."

Paul leveled a steady look on Evan. "I sent her away—" he began. Heads turned, eyebrows lifted. "—in order to insure her safety."

He received several incredulous looks.

"Safety from what?" Jennifer demanded. "Us?"

Paul let silence be his answer.

Jennifer drew a shocked breath.

"Someone," Paul explained, "took exception to her being here. She didn't fall into the lake yesterday. She was pushed."

Jennifer stabbed a piece of meat with her fork. "And you automatically blame us! Paul, I'm beginning to worry about you! You have a persecution complex that won't quit."

"Who else should I blame?" Paul asked. "Who else has such good reasons?"

"Well I, for one, don't believe it," Jean Anne pronounced. "It was probably just her imagination. None of us would do a thing like that!"

"Absolutely not!" Dusty concurred, offended.

Paul smiled slightly. "If someone killed Oriel in cold blood, why not her sister?"

The shock of his words echoed in the room. It was a moment before any of them could react. Then, falling over themselves, the protests came:

"My God! Surely you don't *mean* that!"

"Oriel *killed?*"

"What proof do you have?"

"How can you say that?"

"Why, you sanctimonious..."

Frank, who had been silent, lifted his wineglass. "I was wondering when someone was finally going to raise that question. Everyone accepted Oriel's 'accident' so easily... *too* easily."

Mary LeBlanc recoiled. "But *murder?*" she cried.

Frank smiled. "Well, you do have to admit that it looks suspicious. Oriel, through her father, had a stranglehold on all of us. All of us wanting to be free. What simpler way than for one of us to 'arrange' a little accident?"

"That's just like you, Frank," Jean Anne snipped nastily. "Taking his side over ours!"

"I'm not taking anyone's side, except Oriel's."

"What absolves you?" Jennifer angrily challenged him. "You had just as much to gain as the rest of us. And you went to see her the day she died. The fire started only a few hours after you left."

"Dusty and I were in Oregon," Jean Anne inserted anxiously. "The whole day. Neither of us could have—"

Frank gave Jean Anne a withering look before turning to answer Jennifer's question. "That's right. It did."

"A little gasoline in the right place—" Roger speculated, his eyes narrowing.

"This isn't a film, Roger," Frank chided. "Anyway, if there was even the slightest trace of gasoline around, the police would have found it."

"I don't want to hear this!" Evan commanded from the head of the table. "If the police said it was an accident, it was an accident! Leave it at that!"

"Don't you want to know the truth?" Paul challenged smoothly. "What are you afraid of?"

Evan straightened. "I'm afraid of nothing!"

"*You* had more to gain than the rest of us, Evan," Jim Clark accused. Jennifer nodded.

"That still doesn't mean that I..."

Frank slammed his fist down hard on the table, seizing everyone's attention, causing Evan's words to freeze.

He looked slowly from face to face. "I know what you think of me. I don't think much better of myself. I have a lot of failings. But no one can say I'm not loyal. I remember Oriel as a child. I remember her growing into an adult. I remember how her father treated her, giving her love one minute and withholding it the next. I know how deeply she loved him, hated him, wanted to please him. I *know* what he did to her." His gaze settled on Paul. "You think of me as a drunk, a misfit, a parasite. You hate me because I loved her, and because once, she loved me. But it's because I loved her, that I wasn't satisfied with the police report. I carried out my own investigation." His gaze traveled the table. "Anyone interested in what I found out?"

All eyes were on him, fascinated by the prospect that one of their own could be guilty.

"It was an accident," Frank said softly after a suspenseful moment. "Purely and simply an accident. I have a friend who works in the arson department of another major city. He confirmed the first report. There was faulty wiring in the wing where Oriel was sleeping. There was an ignition, and Oriel died, along with several others. I have his report, if anyone would like to see it. And I'll be happy to give you his name and number and any number of references."

Jean Anne shivered. "No thanks, I believe you." Then she looked slyly at Paul. "But Paul doesn't."

Paul watched Frank steadily. "I believe him," he said quietly. "In this. I'm not so sure where it concerns Allison."

Frank blinked. The others tensed again.

"Who's Allison?" Roger asked. "We don't know any Allison."

Paul didn't remove his gaze from Frank, who had started to smile, the lines at the corners of his eyes crinkling deeply.

"Allison," Frank explained, "is the woman impersonating Magda. I knew she was an impostor from the instant I saw her."

"You seemed to," Paul agreed. "But I doubt that you were very confident. What happened, Frank? Did you just snap? You couldn't take it anymore, so you thought you'd solve everyone's problem with a little shove? Then when she didn't die you hurried back, pretending to be drunk—that should be easy for you,

you've had so much practice—and pretended to rescue her?"

Frank was calm in the face of his accusation. "My conscience is clear. I liked Allison too much to want to harm her."

Jean Anne's lip curled. "You're very attached to her, Paul. Is she your lover or something?"

Paul ignored her. He looked carefully at the others. "More than a little impatient...couldn't wait. Get rid of the problem before it became a bigger one. Is that the way it was? Follow her, wait for an opportunity, then when she's standing at the end of the rocks, give her a little shove—"

"Your case won't hold water," Dusty commented smugly. "If none of us killed Oriel, why would one of us want to kill Mag—this Allison person?"

"Because you'd had a taste of freedom and didn't want it taken away. She posed a threat."

"You have an answer for everything," Mary Le-Blanc complained bitterly. "Can't you just be satisfied that your little friend only received a slight bump on the head?"

Paul's gaze settled on Mary. For as long as he had known her, he had marveled that her bland looks were so misleading. Like a spider, she hid her poisonous venom behind an ordinary facade. "Did I say anything about a bump on her head?"

Mary instantly recognized her mistake. Her face paled and then flushed, and she looked at Paul with a hatred he'd never seen before. Leaping up from the table, she sprinted the distance between them and started to flail at him, hitting him about the head and shoulders with her fists. All the while, she was screeching and calling him every obscene name she could think of.

At first Dusty was slow to react. Shock held him to his seat. But after a moment, being the closest male, he jumped to his feet and tried to pin Mary's arms. Evan was second to arrive, followed quickly by Jennifer. It took the three of them to pull her off of Paul.

"You bastard!" she spat. "Yes, I did it! And I'd do it again! We've waited too long, Roger and me. Too, too long! First Damien, then Oriel and next *Magda?* It was too much . . . just too, too *much!*"

Roger hadn't moved. He just sat there looking stunned.

Evan glanced at him impatiently. "Come on, man. Help us! Mary . . . stop it!"

Mary continued to thrash, continued to spew disgusting epithets. Only now the invective was directed at all of them, not just Paul.

Finally Roger stirred himself to intervene. "Mary has had some difficulties lately," he said quietly after he had swept her into his arms. "But I didn't think it would carry this far." He glanced at Dusty. "Could you get the door, please?"

Mary protested vehemently as her husband started to walk away, but when he didn't stop and they entered the hall her screeches changed to tears and copious apologies.

Evan straightened his jacket and tie and ran a smoothing hand over his hair. Then he retook his seat at the head of the table. Dusty and Jennifer followed suit. Faces were more sober than they had been in a long time.

"Poor Mary," Jean Anne murmured.

"Poor Roger!" Jennifer countered.

"It must be awful to lose your mind," Jean Anne mused after a short moment. Then she started to giggle. "Especially when you don't have all that much to lose in the first place!"

Dusty looked startled, then grinned, joining in with his girlfriend's twisted sense of humor. "It's not as if she contributed much to the conversation."

"She's almost as quiet as you are!" Jennifer teased, looking slyly at her husband. "Are you going to slip off into lala land next, Jim darling?"

"It's the quiet ones who have to be watched!" Evan quipped, not content to be left out.

Frank sat quietly in his place at the table, listening to the exchange. When he looked up, he met Paul's gaze. Understanding passed between the two men. Neither belonged to this group. But there was a subtle difference between them. Paul meant to leave, never to return. As far as Frank was concerned, they were still his closest friends, and warts and all he would remain with them. He lifted his glass in a silent salute and took a long sip.

Paul turned away, disgusted by the general behavior but not surprised by it. He wanted to leave this house as fast as he could.

Evan stopped him.

"Why did you do it?" he asked curiously. "Did you suspect one of us from the beginning? Is that why you brought that woman here and set her up as Magda?"

"I suspected nothing," Paul answered.

"Then why did you do it?"

"Because I wanted to watch you squirm."

Evan nodded at the directness of the answer. It was something he could understand. "I should tell you," he said. "I heard from my investigator about an hour ago. He'd made his way to the island, stormed the convent and learned that Magda never lived there. Then he did a little more checking— I told you he was good—and he discovered that Magda, the *real* Magda, died on one of the other islands when she was about fourteen. She and her mother, in some kind of boating accident."

"So you truly are free," Paul said.

Evan had the honesty not to evade. "Yes," he said simply. "We are."

A joyful shout emerged from farther down the table. Glasses were lifted, laughter exchanged...and Paul quickly left the room.

Just as he had originally thought—not one of them mourned Oriel. Except maybe Frank. All that mattered to the rest was what they stood to receive. In their

minds, at this moment, they were free. But was anyone ever completely free? Free from one's self?

Paul felt a hollowness deep inside. A chapter in his
life had closed. A long chapter with many headings.

He had no idea what was going to come next.

Chapter Fourteen

The hollowness that Paul experienced at the house on Lake Tahoe continued like a vacuum in his soul once he returned to the city. He felt nothing. Absolutely nothing. He was numb.

Whenever he thought of Oriel, which was less often as the weeks went by, it was as if she was a fictional character. As if somehow they had *all* been fictional characters... including himself.

He worked, he ate, he slept—repeating the process day after day. His life held nothing more. It was empty.

Randall considered him across the café table, taking in the gaunt appearance, the shell-shocked eyes, the nervous tapping of his fingers on the fine linen tablecloth.

"Relax, Paul! Enjoy yourself. I thought you liked opera."

"I do. Some of it."

"Well? What's more fun than *The Mikado*?"

Paul looked away from his friend, the window seat allowing him to gaze across the busy intersection. "You should have asked someone else. I'm not the best company these days."

Randall sighed. "I asked you because I thought you needed entertaining. I guarantee you're not my first choice for a date."

Paul smiled slightly.

Randall leaned back in his chair. "Actually, I would have asked Allison, but her grandfather is coming home from the hospital tomorrow and she has quite a few things to do tonight."

Paul's head lifted. "Allison?"

"Yes."

Paul was silent. Then: "How is she?"

"Fine. She went through a hard time. For a bit it was touch-and-go. But her grandfather seems to be fairly tough. He started to snap back after a few days. He's lost some mobility on his left side, though. And he'd already lost some brain function. He doesn't know her."

"That's hard."

"Yes."

Paul's feeling of depression increased. "You, ah— You've seen a lot of her?"

"I've helped out from time to time. Dropped her off at the hospital, and so on. She's totally devoted to her grandfather."

"She said he was ill. I didn't believe her."

"Why don't you go see her yourself?" Randall suggested. "She's not gone back to work yet and she probably won't. Not for a time...thanks to your generosity."

Paul shook his head. "No."

"Why not?"

"Has she asked about me?"

"Well...no."

Paul drew a long breath.

Randall's gray eyes watched him steadily. "What happened in that house, Paul?" he asked. "I know about the attempt on her life...but there was something else, wasn't there?"

"I'd rather not talk about it," Paul evaded.

"Did something happen between the two of you?"

Paul's hand jerked, toppling his fork to the floor. A passing waiter was quick to retrieve it and offer another.

Randall took the pressure off by glancing at his watch. "I guess we'd best be on our way. The first act's due to start in fifteen minutes. We don't want to miss it."

Paul followed his friend from the restaurant and walked the short distance to the Opera House. In their tuxedos they made a striking pair: Paul with his dark good looks and Randall seeming to be everyone's ideal of the boy-next-door.

Randall commented from time to time during the next few hours, but Paul couldn't have told anyone later what he said, just as he couldn't have summed up the operetta without having witnessed other versions several times before.

ONCE AGAIN IN THE LONELINESS of his home, Paul looked at the slip of paper Randall had given him. It contained Allison's address and telephone number.

Paul held on to the abbreviated sheet, unwilling to put it down. With that one small connection, he had suddenly realized what had been happening to him: while on one level all his thoughts, all his feeling had been suspended, underneath they were shifting, changing, evolving! Oriel was Oriel and he still cared deeply for her, but he could see now that the love he felt for her could never be. He had loved her like she was some kind of goddess and he the willing suppliant. She was perfect, unattainable. A young boy's ideal of love, not a man's. A man needed warmth and compassion and tenderness. Loyalty and honesty and fire.

Allison!

Paul stood as if paralyzed.

It was Allison who was warm and compassionate and tender, and who saw that people had different facets. It was Allison who had responded so passionately each time he had come to her...seeing Oriel, but also somehow seeing her. Even if he hadn't been aware of it, a part of him had always sensed that she was different from Oriel. Otherwise, he wouldn't have gone to her. She looked like Oriel, but he could touch her...kiss her...make love to her. Something he could never do with the real Oriel. So he *had* to have sensed a difference.

And he had sent her away. In the name of safety? Yes. But was it also because he sensed that his obsession with Oriel was at an end and that he was beginning to see Allison for the woman that she really was? Had the idea unnerved him? He hadn't known who he was anymore after Oriel. He'd had to take time. He'd had to heal.

Now that time was over.

He looked at the slip of paper held tightly in his hand and without a second thought headed smartly for the door.

ALLISON DUSTED THE LAST piece of furniture in her grandfather's room. She had been cleaning the apartment since late afternoon and still had the bathroom to go before she was done. She was leaving that to the last so that she could shower and change into her gown and then fall into bed. She was exhausted from her long vigil at the hospital, but she wanted everything to be immaculate for her grandfather's return. He wouldn't notice, but there was so little she could do for him these days that any small service felt rewarding.

She gazed about the simple room, her eyes alighting on her grandfather's favorite hat and favorite painting, hanging side by side on the wall. The painting was of a three-masted schooner, battered yet still battling valiantly against a raging storm. It reminded her of the storm her grandfather had just survived and the way he had battled back, something she had been afraid wouldn't happen the first few days after leaving Lake Tahoe... and Paul.

Paul. Merely thinking his name brought on a hurtful pang—causing, as it did, memories of the times when they had been closest: when his lips had moved hungrily against hers, when his hands had roamed the contours of her body, when he had looked at her with those burning eyes filled with love... and seen Oriel.

Allison uttered a small cry. The weeks had not lessened her pain. Throughout her grandfather's hospital stay, throughout her distress and anguish... It hurt to be reminded of how little she meant to him. That she was nothing in his life.

Allison gathered her cleaning materials and started for the storage cabinet where she planned to exchange furniture polish and dusting cloth for the stronger cleansers to be used in the bathroom. She had just opened the cabinet door when the doorbell rang.

She frowned. She expected no one. Mrs. Beaumont was still at her nephew's home, helping to care for him and his family—she had talked with her only that day. Anyway, it was late. She checked her watch. It was after midnight.

Her frown deepened as the doorbell rang again. Her instinct was to pretend that she wasn't at home. She never made a habit of opening her door in the daytime, much less at night, without being sure just who was on the other side.

She waited, her breath suspended.

Knuckles rapped on wood.

Allison glanced at the phone, wondering if she would have to use it. Then a man's voice called, "Allison?"

She didn't recognize it.

"Allison, please," he said. "I need to talk to you."

It was Paul! Fire and ice shot through her veins. She started to panic. What was he doing here? What did he want? How did he know where she lived?

"Allison?" he called again.

Allison couldn't move. She felt frozen to the spot. She couldn't believe that he was truly there. It was only when she heard him start to move away that she was able to croak, "Paul?"

His retreating steps stopped. "Allison?"

She hadn't recognized his voice when he said her name because she had never heard him use it! Sometimes she had even wondered if he remembered what it was! Allison's heart gave a tiny little leap.

"What—what do you want?" she asked. "How did you find me?"

"Randall gave me your address."

"Is he with you?"

"No, it's just me. Allison? Do you think you could let me inside?"

Allison looked down at her torn jeans and scruffy sweatshirt. While cleaning, she usually wore her oldest clothes. And her hair, once clasped neatly on top of her head in a twisted knot, had started to fall, strand by strand, until now more was down than up.

Her hands fluttered to the stragglers, attempting to discipline them, but she soon gave up.

"Allison?" he repeated.

"Just—just a minute," she called. She ridded herself of her supplies and glanced quickly about the apartment. She was glad that she had cleaned the living room first. In no way was it a match for Paul's house or for Oriel's mansion at the lake, but at least it was tidy.

She stepped to the door and undid the latch. Slowly she opened it to see Paul standing on the landing, breathtakingly handsome in formal black and white. Her eyes glided over him...over his features. It seemed so long since she had seen him!

His smile came and went. "Hello," he said.

Allison's body was taut as she stood aside to let him enter. Once inside, his gaze quickly went about the room, taking in its cramped size and tattered but clean appearance.

Allison felt awkward in his presence. Awkward about any comparisons he might make. "What do you want?" she asked stiffly, not exactly friendly.

Paul's gaze came to settle on her. "Randall told me about your grandfather. I—I came by to offer you that bonus I promised. You certainly earned it."

"I don't want your money. I'm fine."

"But you wouldn't be if Mary had hit you a little harder. She..."

"Mary?" Allison echoed, shocked. "It was Mary?"

Paul nodded. "She's been having emotional trouble lately."

"Haven't we all," Allison murmured.

"Roger's been trying to get her to accept treatment. Now I'm sure she will." Paul searched for something more to say. He felt odd about having come here so precipitously. It was after midnight. But he had wanted to see her and he had driven here like a compass needle finding north. It was only at the last minute that he had come up with an excuse. He now fell back upon it gratefully.

"That's why I want to give you the bonus. Like I said, you earned it."

"But I don't need your money," she insisted.

"I understand your grandfather will require a nurse."

"He already has a nurse. Two, in fact. The two I hired to take care of him while I was with you at the lake." At his look of surprise, she added, "You gave me half the money up front, remember? Anyway, I plan to take care of him myself during the day, at least for a while. That will cut down on some of the expense."

"Then let me cover the fee for the night nurse. I'm sure you must have other places to put . . ."

"I don't *need* your money!"

"Don't be stubborn," he chided, feeling that he needed to do something.

"Don't tell me what to be!" she flared. "I don't work for you any longer!"

"But I'd like to help you! It could be the one decent thing to come out of this whole stupid mess!"

Allison took a calming breath. "Look, I knew what I was doing when I went with you. I knew that those people weren't going to make my life easy! I'd have been a fool not to realize it. So would you."

"But I never thought you'd be in danger. If I had..."

"You'd have done exactly the same thing. You never cared a thing about me, Paul. All you wanted was revenge."

"And I was wrong! I know I was wrong. Now all I want to do is help you."

"Why?" she demanded. "Because I still remind you of Oriel?"

"No! It's because—" Paul didn't know what to say. He hadn't thought it through far enough. He thought he knew, but— Words suddenly spilled from him. "It's because I want to be with you! I want to see you! I don't know why. I just—"

Allison sank down into the nearest chair. She had to because her legs wouldn't support her any longer.

Paul raked a hand through his hair. He was as disturbed by his outburst as she was.

"I don't believe you," Allison whispered. "It's because you're still focused on her. I look like her...you get us confused. You always have."

"That's not true! Not anymore. I know you for who you are now. Not for who you aren't."

Allison again brushed the stray strands of hair away from her face and thought rather sardonically that at times life had a rather funny way of unfolding. Not five minutes before she had been contemplating cleaning the bathroom and then falling into bed to sleep, with the most exciting prospect of her evening being to turn out her light!

"My grandfather is coming back from the hospital tomorrow," she said at last. "That's all I can think about right now. That's where all my energy has to go. I can't—I can't be distracted by anything else."

"You don't believe me," Paul said.

"Do you blame me?"

"How can I prove it?" he urged.

"I don't know."

Paul hesitated. "May I see you again?"

"I have to stay with my grandfather."

"Not at night. You said you'd have a night nurse."

"I'll be tired by then. There's so much to do each day."

"Then I'll help you. I'll come every afternoon."

"Here?"

"What time is he checking out of the hospital?"

"Eleven, but—"

"Would you like me to drive?"

"Paul!"

"I have to be with you, Allison. I don't have everything straightened out yet. But I do know that."

Allison trembled. "Randall's—Randall's stopping by. A friend of mine was going to do it, but she had to cancel. Randall's really been a big help while Grand-dad was in the hospital. Especially the first few days."

Randall! Paul received a nasty jolt. "Then I'll be here at one. You can show me what to do."

"But—"

"No buts. I'm doing it."

Allison met his determined gaze.

In silence, she agreed.

RANDALL WAS STILL at Allison's house when Paul arrived the next afternoon.

"We had a delay," Allison explained. "The doctor had an emergency and he was running late."

Paul nodded, eyeing his friend, trying to gauge the extent of affairs between him and Allison. Like a hawk he watched as Randall helped by making coffee and then seated himself comfortably on her couch, a comfort that could only come from familiarity.

"You're early, aren't you?" Randall asked as Allison went to check on her grandfather.

"I got through with my work ahead of time," Paul said.

Allison returned to perch on the edge of a sofa cushion, looking tired and tense. "He's still sleeping," she said worriedly. "I'm not sure if he even knows he's been moved."

"That's probably for the best," Randall comforted.

Allison dipped her head, took a sip of coffee, then pushed the cup away. "I still wish I'd been here when he—" She bit her bottom lip.

"You couldn't have changed anything," Randall said.

"No, but—" Allison glanced at Paul and immediately stopped speaking. A moment later she drew a breath. "I don't blame you, Paul. It wasn't your fault. It would have happened whether I was here or not. It's just—"

"If I could change things, I would," Paul said quietly.

Allison hurried to her grandfather's room again, thinking that she had heard a noise. Once she had gone, Randall leaned forward to say softly, "You care a great deal for her, don't you?"

Paul was startled by his friend's perceptiveness. "Is it obvious?"

"To a good friend, yes."

"She doesn't believe it."

"It's been a hard few weeks. Maybe she will when things settle down a bit."

"She thinks I still get her confused with Oriel."

"And do you?"

"No. Not anymore." Paul leveled a dark look. "What about you? How serious is it for you?"

"I care for her. But not in the way you mean."

Paul heaved a sigh.

Randall smiled slightly in amusement. "I had a feeling I knew what was bothering the two of you."

"Two?" Paul was quick to pick up on the word.

Allison returned at that moment, breaking into whatever Randall had been going to say. "It must have come from outside. Granddad hasn't moved." She looked from one man to the other. "Did I interrupt something?"

Paul immediately sat back. "No, not really." He tried to sound blasé, but it didn't come off very well. She looked at him curiously.

Randall stood up. "I have to go. I have several things to see to this afternoon. Allison, you know if you need me, all you have to do is call."

Allison took his hand. "Yes, I know. And thank you . . . for everything."

Randall returned her smile, then glancing at Paul, said, "I suppose I'll be talking to you another time?"

"I'll call."

Allison saw Randall to the door, and when she came back she returned to her perch on the couch. But she wasn't comfortable. She looked at her hands, she rearranged her coffee cup, she glanced at Paul and then away again.

Paul, too, was at a loss. So much between them remained unspoken. They had met under odd circumstances, they had dealt with each other under odd circumstances...and if what Randall had hinted at was true, it was possible that they had come to fall in love under odd circumstances. Most people start their relationships with idle chitchat before progressing to anything else. They had totally skipped that part. Instinctively Paul knew that they needed to experience it in order to become comfortable with each other, but it was far easier to acknowledge a problem than find the solution. He racked his brain for something to say and could find only blankness.

"How long have you known Randall?" Allison asked at last, interrupting what seemed a long silence.

"Since college. We were roommates."

"Which college?"

"Stanford."

Allison nodded.

Paul was relieved to have something to talk about, even if it was Randall. "He was a whiz at mathematics. At first he thought about becoming a physicist, but he became interested in law during his junior year and switched majors. He's been on his way up ever since."

"What about you?" she asked.

He shrugged. "My interests drifted for a time but I ended up majoring in business."

"Doing what?"

"I sell real estate. Commercial real estate. My partner and I worked for another company for a time, then we started our own firm."

"You sell buildings?"

"Some big ones, some small ones...we also put together leasing agreements."

"Do you enjoy it?"

"Most of the time. There are moments when I wouldn't mind chucking it all and moving to Tahiti, but those are rare."

"It must keep you busy."

"The hours were long at first, especially when we were trying to get established. But now we have other people to help us."

"Is that how you could afford so much time off?"

Paul smiled. "The perks of being a boss."

If he had thought that answer was going to reassure her, he quickly discovered that it didn't. If anything, she became even more tense.

Paul frowned. "Allison? What's wrong? What did I...?"

Allison stood up. He didn't know it, but he had just underscored one of the major differences in their lives. He was at the top of the work force; she was near the bottom. "I know you say you want to help," she said fretfully. "But please, for today, just go. I don't have the energy for company right now. I'm tired and—"

"I'm not company," he interjected.

"Please!" Allison cried.

The anxiety in her voice cut Paul to the quick. He was here to help her, not make life more difficult. He got to his feet. "All right. I'll go," he said. "But I'll be back. It's not like what you said at the house, Allison—I'm not like the others. At least I'm trying not to be."

Allison remembered the accusation she had hurled at him shortly before departing. That he remembered it surprised her.

This time a sound came from her grandfather's room and caused Allison to start. She glanced at the partially closed door and then back at Paul. There were tears in her soft green eyes.

Paul swallowed tightly. He didn't want to leave her like this! He wanted to stay with her, talking to her, discovering everything that he could about her. Letting her get to know him. But he didn't raise another protest because she had asked him to leave. And he would do anything that she asked, short of never seeing her again. He knew he could never promise that.

Chapter Fifteen

Paul sat at his desk, his chair turned so that he could stare out the window. Just by chance his view overlooked the street where Allison lived and if he tipped his head, he could see her actual building. Or at least he thought he could.

In the week during which he had been helping her, little work had been accomplished. All he could do was think of her. His time in the office was spent waiting, the minutes dragging by. If she would welcome his early arrival, he would leave now. But he knew that he had to prove himself. Each day, as agreed, he arrived promptly at two and left promptly at six. And each day, while they cared for her grandfather, they learned more about one another.

He'd had no idea that she had lost her mother when she was a child or that her father had abandoned her to her grandfather's care at approximately the same age as he had lost his parents. And that as a child she, too, had felt the weight of guilt—as if she was responsible for what had happened.

She'd also told him about her grandfather, of the time when he was healthy and strong. About their initial tug of wills and then the growing love. But Paul hadn't needed to be told of her love for the older man. He had seen it for himself. In the way she looked at him with her soft green eyes. In the way she patiently helped him eat, helped him dress, as well as the way she talked to him, uncaring that he didn't respond. He also admired the way she tried to keep the atmosphere in their home happy. The way she cheered her grandfather's negligible efforts at physical therapy.

"That's the way, Granddad! Squeeze my fingers tight. You can do it! You wouldn't want Dr. Johnson to think that we've been goofing off, would you? Squeeze. Squeeze. That's it!"

But whether or not she had succeeded with her grandfather, she had succeeded with him. Because in that moment he had realized that he had been witness to a great generosity of spirit that was willing to give even when faced with no reward. And it was then that he sorted out a final piece of the puzzle that remained. Oriel had been generous, but only with her money. Allison had little money, but she was generous with herself. Allison *was* what he had only imagined Oriel to be.

And then suddenly he realized: he loved her. Truly loved her. It wasn't obsession or infatuation; he knew the difference now. It wasn't because of the way she looked. Because as the days went by, he had begun to see differences—the way a person who loved an identical twin could never be fooled by the other. It was something *inside* Allison that set her apart.

The problem that now confronted him was that he hadn't always been able to see that difference. And she knew it. If he told her now that he loved her, she would reject the idea even more vehemently than she had rejected his first offer of assistance. So he kept his feelings to himself, as hard as that was to do, and watched as she spent all her love on her grandfather.

Paul checked his watch and swiveled his chair impatiently. He was ready to be on his way; ready to be with her.

He didn't begrudge her grandfather her love, though. From everything he had heard about the man, he respected him and was grateful to him for what he had done for Allison.

At times he wondered how his life would have been different if he had been sent to a loving grandfather instead of into the swirling poisons of the Woodrich home. If instead of watching the other boys at his boarding school leave with their parents for session holidays and summer breaks, he'd had a loving family to return to. He remembered how badly he had missed his own parents and yearned to belong to a real family. Now he wanted it again.

A tap sounded on his door, soon followed by Randall's wide-open smile.

Paul had swung his chair around and now swung it back.

Randall walked straight to the window to follow the direction of Paul's gaze.

"Ah...I thought so. You have a better view. My building faces a little too far to the left."

"What do you want, Randall?" Even though his friend had denied interest, Paul remained unsure of his true feelings for Allison. Sometimes he still wondered...

Randall stepped back to hitch a seat on the corner of Paul's desk. "Well, I just happen to have two tickets to the last performance of *The Mikado*. A client of mine gave them to me. I didn't have the heart to tell her that I'd already seen it. She thought she was doing me a gigantic favor. It's sold out, you know."

"Why are you telling me this? Why don't you just call someone and go. You're not asking me to be your date again, are you?"

Randall grinned. "Nope. Once was enough. I like my dates shaped better."

Paul couldn't prevent a grin. He turned the chair a little more toward his friend. "So I'm still asking. Why are you telling me?"

Randall tapped the tickets lightly on his thigh. "Because I thought maybe I'd give them to you. And you could take Allison."

Paul shook his head. "She won't go. She won't leave her grandfather."

"Not even with the nurse...and me?"

"You?" Paul repeated.

Randall's grin widened. "Just call me Cupid!"

Paul pulled the tickets from his fingers. "When is this last performance?"

"Tonight."

"Now I *know* she won't go."

"I've already asked her."

"You've what?" Paul was stunned.

"Well, someone had to take a hand. For a person who knew exactly what he was doing and was hell-bent to get there, you've certainly changed, Paul. You don't seem to know whether you're coming or going anymore. You just sit here, day after day, staring morosely out that window. I know, because Doris told me."

"Remind me to tell Doris to keep her mouth shut."

"She's the best secretary you've ever had, so don't alienate her."

Paul looked at the tickets. "Allison said she'd come? Just like that?"

"Well, I did neglect to mention that you'd be taking my place. But that's a small oversight. She'll adjust."

Paul closed his eyes. "Randall, one day—"

"She loves you, Paul." His friend was suddenly serious.

"You're the only person I've ever heard say that."

"Give her time. Give yourself time. What happened before was a little...unusual, but it can be overcome."

"I wish I'd listened to you."

"You did what you felt you had to do at the time. I thought you were crazed, but basically I trusted your good judgment. Otherwise I'd have locked you up somewhere."

"I hurt her. I didn't mean to do it, but I did."

"Then try not to hurt her again."

"She's not at all like Oriel. She's kind and sweet and..."

"I know! I know her, too, remember?" He pushed away from the desk. "I'll be at the apartment at seven-thirty. You can tell her ahead or not, whatever you think."

"She'll be suspicious when I turn up in a tux and you're dressed in jeans."

Randall grinned. "Hey...I provided the tickets. The rest is up to you!"

"Thanks."

"Don't mention it," Randall teased and slipped out of the room.

ALLISON GLANCED AT THE kitchen clock. It was already well past two and Paul had not yet arrived. She frowned slightly, wondering if something had held him up.

At three, she received a call. His secretary informed her that he wouldn't be able to come round. She gave no reason, no excuse. Allison hung up, disturbed. She had grown accustomed to Paul's company in the afternoons, accustomed to his presence. He was no longer the cold stranger intent only on his cause. In that man's place was another who showed both strength and gentleness as he helped care for her grandfather. A man whose slow smile she would be unable to live without.

At four, the doorbell rang, drawing Allison away from preparations for her grandfather's evening meal. A delivery man waited and in his arms was a large, flat box.

Allison stared at it and then at him. "You must have the wrong address. I didn't order anything." Left unsaid was the additional: not from *that* store, ever! The box bore the name of one of the exclusive shops on Union Square.

"Is this...?" He named her address. "And are you...?" He read her name.

"Yes," Allison gulped.

"Then it's for you, lady. All you have to do is sign for it."

Allison scrawled a signature that wouldn't have held up in a court of law.

The box was thrust into her arms, whereupon the man hustled down the stairs, jumped into a small van and sped away.

Allison slowly closed the door and sank onto the couch, the box resting on her lap. With trembling fingers, she opened it. Inside, cushioned by clouds of tissue paper, was one of the most beautiful dresses she had ever seen! It was snow white, delicate and soft, with tiny pink, blue and pale yellow flowers clustered at the left shoulder before dipping in a graceful curve to the fitted waist. When she lifted it, she saw that its length was formal and that it had a matching wrap.

For a moment all Allison could do was stare at it. Then she saw the envelope. Her fingers shook even more as she found the card inside. The words were lyrics from a popular Broadway musical:

A thousand years might pass unknown,
Until the day that you were born...
Then all the earth grew hushed and quiet,
Waiting for your perfect song

"Allison, your song is soft and indescribably sweet, a reflection of the gentleness of your soul. Please accept this small offering from someone who cares."

The card was unsigned. Allison read it again...and again. The words were beautiful enough to bring tears to her eyes. *Someone who cares...*

Randall? Had Randall sent the dress? He was the only person who knew that she might need one. He had asked her to the operetta tonight. But the words had more intensity of feeling than she expected from Randall. He liked her; he cared for her. But he didn't love her. Not as a man loves a woman. Not as...

Paul! Did Paul know? He had bought dresses for her before, the ones she had used as Magda, the dresses she had given to a charity sale the day after she returned to San Francisco because she couldn't bear to look at them any longer. He knew her size....

Joy leapt in Allison's heart. Because if this dress was from Paul, it showed a new depth of feeling, of realization. If he could buy a dress like this, one of such simple beauty—for her!—then it meant that his view of her had really changed. As he had told her that it had. As she had been afraid to believe.

Allison lifted the dress and hugged it to her breast.

AT THE APPOINTED TIME Allison was waiting. She had called the night nurse in early and taken an extra hour to get ready. But while preparing for the evening she had tempered her excitement. It was still possible that the dress had been sent by Randall. He was such a special person; thoughtful as well as enjoyable to be around. And if he had sent the dress, she would try not to act disappointed. She didn't want to hurt his feelings. But if it was from Paul, she would know tonight. Randall would tell her.

When the doorbell rang she jumped, her nerves stretched taut. Fixing a smile and readying words of welcome, she went to answer it. Only to have the words instantly dry and her knees turn to water, as Paul, magnificent again in his tux, stood outside the door.

His dark eyes swept over her, taking in the way she looked, showing quiet satisfaction. And there was something else—the something that made her knees buckle.

"You look beautiful," he said quietly.

"So do you," she whispered and he smiled.

"The dress fits perfectly."

"Yes—thank you."

The question was answered. Allison wanted to throw herself into his arms but held back. Paul didn't move.

How long they would have continued to stand there, facing each other in the doorway, Allison had no idea, because she had no concept of time passing. Not until Randall interrupted them. He was dressed in jeans and a sweater pulled over a shirt. "Sorry I'm late," he said. "I had a little trouble with the elevator in my building. Thought I was going to spend the night in it." He looked from one to the other. "Is there a reason why we're standing in the hall?"

Allison jerked to awareness, stepping back, inviting them both to enter. Randall clapped Paul on the back and motioned him in ahead.

"You two look sensational," he said. "I suppose Paul's told you I'm not going... that you'll have to make do with him. You don't mind, do you? I thought I'd take Nurse Hunter on in a hot game of gin as soon as she settles your grandfather for the night. She told me she was a gin addict the other day and so am I. You don't mind, do you?"

Allison shook her head.

"Good," he said, rubbing his hands together. "Because I can't wait!"

"You don't have to do this, Randall," Allison said. "I trust Mrs. Hunter completely."

"It's no sacrifice. See—" He pulled out a deck of cards. "I came prepared."

The nurse came out of Allison's grandfather's room and smiled when she saw Randall, then her thin face brightened even more when she saw the cards, the lines of age smoothing.

"I'll set things up for later," Randall told her. Then to Allison and Paul, "Why don't you two get going. Everything will be fine here."

"I'd like to say good-night to my grandfather," Allison said. "I won't be long."

She slipped into the bedroom at the same time as the nurse returned.

"I'll just be a second," she said before kneeling at her grandfather's side. He was propped up in bed, having been moved recently from a nearby chair. His eyes were blank, turned completely in on himself.

Allison touched his hand, smoothing the aged skin. "I'm going out for a while, Granddad," she said softly. "Just for a little while. I won't be long. I love you."

He began to rock the upper portion of his body and hum a tune she didn't recognize. Then, startling her, he turned to look straight at her and smiled into her eyes. Just as he used to do before he became ill. All too soon, though, the smile disappeared and he was once again in his private world.

"He smiled!" Allison breathed, stunned.

She leaned close to look at him, to see if any telltale sign remained. She called his name, but he gave no notice.

She looked at the nurse. "He smiled at me. He really did! He knew me!"

Allison kissed her grandfather's cheek before rushing into the other room where the two men were waiting. "Granddad smiled at me!" she cried excitedly. "He looked at me and smiled. It was just for a second, but it was real! Isn't that wonderful?"

Allison laughed and wiped at her lashes where tears of happiness had collected.

"Would you rather stay home tonight?" Paul asked quietly.

Allison hesitated. She was unsure.

"He's drifting off to sleep again, miss," the nurse said. "Why don't you go out, take a little break. I'm sure you need it."

Allison glanced at Paul. She saw that he would not pressure her in any way. If she wanted to stay home, they would. If not... She glanced at Randall and he smiled encouragement.

She reached for her purse. "Let's go," she said decisively. "If it happened once, it will happen again. I *know* it will!"

ALLISON'S WALK SHOWED both happiness and excitement as they walked from the parking garage to the Opera House. Her face mirrored her elation.

"He knew me, Paul!" she repeated. "It wasn't my imagination. He really did! This is something I've been waiting for for ages!" She laughed delightedly and hugged Paul's arm. "I don't expect a lot," she continued, trying to maintain a hold on reality. "I don't expect him to become the person that he was. I know he can't do that. But it means so much, just to know that once in a while he might recognize me. It's like—I don't know. I can't really find the right words."

Paul smiled down into her glowing face. "You're doing a pretty good job."

Allison's smile grew happier. For years it seemed she'd had the weight of responsibility thrust onto her shoulders. She'd had to make all the decisions, handle all the finances, be the breadwinner. Now, for this moment, she wanted only to be happy and carefree...to concentrate on the good things in life. Her grandfather had smiled at her and she was with the man she loved. He had bought her this beautiful dress and... What more could she possibly want?

THROUGHOUT the performance, Paul watched Allison more than he watched the stage. Their seats were located in one of the private balconies that lined the sides of the great old hall, their view of the stage impeccable.

The original *Mikado* by Gilbert and Sullivan was set in a village in Japan, but for this production it had been moved to an English seaside resort in the 1930s.

The costumes were of that period, as were the sets. But the story was unchanged. Yum-Yum still fell in love with her Nanki-Poo, even though she was unwillingly betrothed to her guardian, Ko-Ko, the Lord High Executioner, who was under orders from the Mikado— part god, part king—to execute someone or be executed himself. And the person he persuades to be executed is Nanki-Poo.

The resulting complications were hilarious, the acting and music superior, the singing voices superb. Allison was fascinated by each successive scene and Paul reveled in her laughter, exulted in watching her expressive face, rejoiced in the fact that occasionally she would look at him and wordlessly share her joy. It was all he could do not to pull her into his arms and tell her how much he loved her, right there—in front of everyone. He'd put on a better show than the one on stage!

At the end of the performance, as they filed out slowly in the company of hundreds of other patrons, Allison flashed him a smile and hummed a few bars from one of the better-known songs. Then she laughed and lightly squeezed his fingers. Paul swallowed tightly. He had to tell her soon, but he was afraid. He didn't want to ruin her evening. Or have her tell him that she never wanted to see him again!

To remain in her company longer, once they were back in the car he asked, "Are you hungry?"

"Are you?" she countered.

"Starving!" Paul returned and actually found that he meant it. He had eaten nothing since breakfast that morning. "Me, too," she laughed. "Let's eat!"

The difference in her was remarkable. The quiet, serious young woman was gone; in her place was someone who enjoyed having fun.

In keeping with her mood, Paul took her to a place in North Beach where some of the best Italian food in the city was served. It was informal and crowded and the waiters treated the customers like family.

They ordered a colossal pizza with everything on it and stuffed themselves until they were silly. Without so much as a glass of wine, everything seemed funny. They sat in their booth, giggling and laughing.

Once they were through, again, neither wanted the evening to end, so they collected Paul's car and just drove.

The night air was warm, unusual for the city, the people walking along the sidewalks seeming to enjoy their freedom from coats and jackets.

They drove across the Golden Gate, gazed at the city from the point on the other side of the bay, then returned.

Still they weren't ready for the evening to end and without comment, Paul parked the car at Ocean Beach. He knew the moment was fast approaching. He couldn't keep silent forever. At least now, if she rejected him, they would have this evening to remember. He opened the passenger's door and held out his hand.

Allison responded eagerly. Something was coming. She had felt it all evening...like a simmering volcano, just beneath the surface of the their enjoyment.

The wind wildly tossed her hair, but instead of trying to tame it, she responded to a reckless urge and let it fly. She was encouraged by the glitter of approval in Paul's eyes.

The Pacific was dimly lighted by a partial moon as they started along the beach, but nothing could mute its power. Wave after wave broke onto shore, creating a faint mist while assaulting the ears.

At another time Allison would have been afraid of ruining her beautiful dress, but this night was enchanted. Like a princess in a fairy tale, she would proceed unscathed.

Paul seemed to have little concern for what he wore, as well, casually removing the formal jacket and hooking it over his shoulder.

Moonlight pearlized her dress and his pleated shirt, just as it highlighted each building wave and resulting explosion of spray and bubbles.

Paul continued to hold her hand and Allison wouldn't have withdrawn it for the world. It served as a vital link between them, something that could be comforting in proper circumstances but was, at this moment, thrilling. She loved the way his hand felt, so different from her own. Larger, stronger, the skin not as soft.

As they walked they said nothing.

Paul was aware that she hadn't pulled her hand away. He was also more than aware of the warmth of her fingers clinging tightly to his, aware of the smoothness of her skin, the intimacy of the small contact. Then she shivered, the balminess of the night having swiftly disappeared at the ocean's edge.

He stopped to place his jacket gently around her shoulders. It easily enveloped Allison's slighter form. It started to slip and instinctively she reached to catch hold of it...but instead of meeting the jacket, her hand came to rest upon his chest.

For a moment neither moved. They stood absolutely still, electrified by what had happened; aware only of each other, their gazes locked.

Then slowly Paul trailed a finger along her cheek and Allison turned her head into the action. An age-old symbol of acceptance.

When she looked up at him, Paul drew a ragged breath. Finally he couldn't stand it any longer. He uttered a soft groan and folded her into his arms.

This time when they kissed, it was different from any time before, full of wonder, with no external forces tearing them apart. They were simply a man and a woman, locked in a heated embrace.

Paul's heart was thundering, his body on fire. He had been blind for so long to what had been evident before his eyes. He couldn't imagine not loving her.

Allison stirred and reluctantly he let her go.

But instead of breaking away, Allison only wanted to cup his face between her hands and look deeply into his eyes.

He met her look, still slightly dazed, but very much in love with her, very much wanting to kiss her again. Obeying instinct, he dipped his head.

She smiled and evaded his lips. "Wait," she whispered.

He pulled back.

She continued to look at him, using the partial light of the moon and stars. Tiny droplets of spray had fastened themselves to his exposed skin, collected on his shirt, on his hair. But she wasn't interested in anything but what she could see in his gaze.

"You truly have put her to rest, haven't you?" she whispered at last.

"Yes," he said huskily. "Do you believe me now?" He needed to hear the words.

"Yes," she said softly in return.

His muscles leaped. "How? Why?" he asked quickly. "What makes this time different?"

"Because you've stopped seeing her when you look at me."

"How can you tell?'

"I could always tell."

Paul pressed closer, trying to regain her lips. If everything was right between them, he didn't want to waste time talking. But Allison stopped him again with the soft touch of her fingertips.

"I'm still not sure if this is right," she said, a light frown clouding her features.

"Why not?" Paul was at once afraid in the midst of joy.

"Because everything about us is so different. You've always had things easy, Paul. I've always had them hard. You've never wanted for anything in your life, except Oriel."

"You're referring to money," he concluded.

"Only people who have money 'refer' to money. The rest of us work for it."

"I'll give everything away! Tomorrow. You can come watch, if you like. I'll meet you at the Civic Center."

"Somehow I can't see you in rags."

Paul unhooked his cummerbund and stamped it into the sand.

Then he slipped off his wisp of a tie and bent to remove his shoes. He was pulling his pleated shirt from his pants when Allison stopped him, giggling.

"I'll keep going," he swore seriously. "Until I'm as naked as the day I was born. Maybe then you'll see me for the man I am. We're no different, Allison. Not underneath. And that's what counts." He took hold of her hand, drawing her back to him. "Don't be as blind as I've been. Don't let the differences between us keep us apart. Having money or not having it doesn't matter between people who care for each other. That's what Oriel didn't understand. She thought money was

power and power was a form of love. That's what got
her so messed up inside.

"Remember what Frank said about love twisting
you as easily as hate? I didn't understand at first, but
I do now. I loved Oriel, or I thought I did. And I
thought I wanted revenge. But I was twisting those
feelings around each other. Hurting other people...hurting you! When I didn't really love her at all.
At least not in the way I thought." He paused, struggling to express his thoughts. "I learned the difference when I fell in love with you. I don't care what you
look like, Allison! I don't care how much money you
have...or don't have! All I care about is you! The
person inside. It's *you* I want to protect, to love, and
to be beside for the rest of my life."

The half-amused smile had faded from Allison's lips
as she absorbed the importance of his words. This day,
if it still was this day and had not spilled over into the
next, had seemed so long. She had moved through so
many experiences.

But the only experience that counted was how much
her life had come to revolve around this man. She
loved him, and now she was satisfied that he truly
loved her...for herself alone. The prospect of Oriel's
ghost was no longer a worry. So why should she continue to object? Yes, there were differences between
them. But wasn't smoothing out differences what living with someone was all about? Loving someone?
Being a part of someone?

"There's one thing," she cautioned, knowing that it had to be said. "My grandfather. I'll always be there for him . . . for as long as he lives. And it wouldn't be fair to ask you to . . ."

"Don't insult me, Allison," he interrupted sternly. "If he's part of your life, he's part of mine."

There was a sudden release of tension in her body. A sudden surrendering of her heart. She and Paul had come together under unusual circumstances. And with the continuing care of her grandfather, they would persist along similar lines. But only one condition between them really mattered: that they loved each other.

The picture they made was interesting. She, in her wonderful white dress with a man's tuxedo jacket pooled carelessly at her feet, her hair a red-gold flame in the moonlight. He, jacketless, with discarded tie and cummerbund, his shirt partially hanging free of his trousers, his stockinged feet planted firmly in the sand a distance away from his forsaken shoes, his dark hair jostled by the wind.

"I love you, Paul," she said softly, looking directly into his eyes.

Then she lost herself in those dark, dark eyes as his head slowly lowered, his lips serving notice of his claim on her for the rest of eternity.

Back by Popular Demand

Janet Dailey
Americana

A romantic tour of America through fifty favorite Harlequin Presents, each set in a different state researched by Janet and her husband, Bill. A journey of a lifetime in one cherished collection.

In July, don't miss the exciting states featured in:

Title #11 — HAWAII
Kona Winds

#12 — IDAHO
The Travelling Kind

Available wherever
Harlequin books are sold.

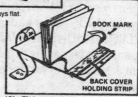

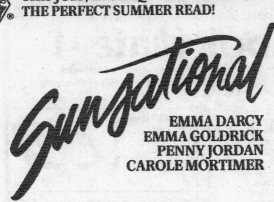